Their gazes met and lo

Something—pheromones, for
between them with an intensi
her knees.

Or was that the wine she'd consumed doing a
number on her?

Perhaps it was both.

Isabella offered him a lighthearted smile. "If you'll
excuse me, I think I'll go to bed."

"Sleep tight."

Yeah, right.

She'd set her sights on finding Mr. Right—or
Señor Right more accurately—but she was afraid
that J.R. Fortune thought he might be that man.

Sure, the city-slicker was handsome—and wealthy.

A very attractive, very appealing man.

But they were as different as night and day.

She'd lost herself and her family roots once, and
she wouldn't allow that to happen again.

That's why she was determined to find the right
mate.

So what was with her growing attraction to the
wrong one?

Dear Reader,

I hope you enjoy *A Real Live Cowboy* as much as I enjoyed writing it and being a part of THE FORTUNES OF TEXAS series.

As an author, I spend a lot of time in my writing cave— or rather, in my office—so it's a joy to participate in a continuity. I love having the opportunity to work with other authors and our editor in creating a series of books with an ongoing story line. In fact, that's one of many reasons I like writing romance for Silhouette Special Edition. Everyone is great to work with!

And taking part in this series was no different. It was fun to revisit Red Rock and some of my favorite characters from the earlier Fortunes of Texas books. I also had the chance to research Fiesta, an actual event that takes place in San Antonio each April. As a result, I'm planning another trip to Texas so that I can experience Fiesta in person.

So sit back and settle into your easy chair with J.R. Fortune and Isabella Mendoza.

Viva Fiesta! And viva romance!

Judy
www.JudyDuarte.com

A REAL LIVE COWBOY

JUDY DUARTE

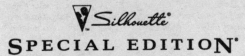

Silhouette

SPECIAL EDITION

Published by Silhouette Books

America's Publisher of Contemporary Romance

Special thanks and acknowledgment to Judy Duarte
for her contribution to
The Fortunes of Texas: Return to Red Rock miniseries.

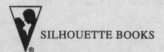

SILHOUETTE BOOKS

ISBN-13: 978-0-373-65446-8
ISBN-10:   0-373-65446-4

Recycling programs
for this product may
not exist in your area.

A REAL LIVE COWBOY

Visit Silhouette Books at www.eHarlequin.com

Printed in U.S.A.

JUDY DUARTE

always knew there was a book inside her. Her dream became a reality in March of 2002, when Silhouette Special Edition released her first book, *Cowboy Courage*. Since then, she has sold more than twenty more novels.

Her stories have touched the hearts of readers around the world. In July of 2005, Judy won the prestigious Readers' Choice Award for *The Rich Man's Son*.

Judy makes her home near the beach in Southern California. When she's not cooped up in her writing cave, she's spending time with her somewhat enormous but delightfully close family.

You can write to Judy c/o Silhouette Books, 233 Broadway, Suite 1001, New York, NY 10237. You can also contact her at JudyDuarte@sbcglobal.net or through her Web site, www.judyduarte.com.

To Marie Ferrarella, Allison Leigh,
Lois Faye Dyer, RaeAnne Thayne and Kristin Hardy
for their contributions to
The Fortunes of Texas: Return to Red Rock series.
It was a pleasure working with you!

And to Susan Litman, whose keen editorial eye kept us
all on track. It's great having such a supportive editor.
You're the best, Susan!

Chapter One

Isabella Mendoza was late, which was *so* not like her.
And to make matters worse, she was the one who'd
insisted on meeting early to avoid the lunch-crowd rush.

As she turned into the driveway that led to Red, the
popular local restaurant, she groaned as she spotted an
all-too-familiar black Cadillac Escalade parked in front.

How was that for luck? Not only did she have to
dash into Red and make apologies to her girlfriend and
her cousins, but with her luck, she would probably run
smack into William Fortune, Jr., better known as J.R. to
everyone in town.

Ever since last week, when he'd officially relocated
from Los Angeles to Red Rock, Texas, their paths had
kept crossing. And to make matters worse, she'd picked
up on the wannabe rancher's obvious interest in her. She

hadn't encouraged him, even if there were plenty of women in town who would have.

Not only was the man wealthy, but he was good-looking, charming and had the kind of body a woman liked to cuddle up next to. But he definitely wasn't Isabella's type.

She parked her red pickup near the side of the building, slid out of the driver's seat and reached for her purse. After securing the lock, she hurried into the restaurant that had once been an old hacienda.

Just four months ago, an arson fire nearly destroyed Red, which had broken Isabella's heart for more reasons than one. Not only did she have a family connection to the owners, José and Maria Mendoza, but she had a deep love and respect for the Tejana culture and the history reflected in the building.

Over the past few months, José and Maria had worked hard to restore the restaurant just the way it was before the fire, although some of the original artwork and antiques had been irreplaceable.

The hostess offered a friendly smile as Isabella walked through the door.

"I'm meeting friends who are already here," Isabella told her.

Out of the corner of her eye, she spotted the back of a tall, broad-shouldered man as he entered the bar, his movements a shadowlike blur. She hadn't gotten a very good look at him, but she had a feeling it was J.R. There was such a solid presence about the man that it was difficult not to notice him. And she had to confess that whenever they were in the same place at the same time, her gaze tended to meet his more often than she liked.

Not that there was anything *wrong* with J.R. The fair-haired businessman-turned-rancher was actually a good catch, if a woman was into Anglos and men who were at least ten years her senior. But that wasn't Isabella, and she had good reason not to get carried away.

Having been raised by her fair-haired stepfather during most of her childhood and adolescence, she had been denied her Tejana heritage, which was why she embraced it now with all her heart and soul. And when she found her Mr. Right, a Latino, he would appreciate her culture as much as she did.

"Your party is on the patio," the hostess said.

Isabella proceeded through the restaurant, her high heels clicking on the Mexican tile floor.

She especially loved Red's courtyard, where water continuously trickled into an Old World–style fountain and brightly colored umbrellas provided shade. The bougainvillea that bloomed in fuchsia, purple and gold weren't as lush and mature as the ones that had adorned the patio before the fire, but they would grow in time.

The women she was meeting—Jane Gilliam, Sierra Calloway, Gloria Fortune and Christina Rockwell—sat at a table near the blue-and-white tiled fountain.

"I'm so sorry I'm late." Isabella took the empty chair between Jane and Christina. "But I have a good excuse. A local businessman stopped by my studio unexpectedly. He owns decorator shops in San Antonio and Houston, and he wants to sell some of my blankets and weavings in both of them."

"That's wonderful," Jane said. "We knew something unexpected must have come up."

"Did you cinch the deal?" Sierra asked.

Isabella smiled, feeling a sense of pride. "Yes. And if I get a few more like that, I'll be able to move my studio out of the garage in my father's backyard and find a more professional place to create and show my work."

"I'd really like to see you move to a cute storefront in Red Rock," Jane said. "It would be so nice to have you working in town. And it would be easier for us to meet for lunch."

Yes, it would be. Jane had become Isabella's closest friend. They'd met last year at Fiesta, a ten-day festival held every April to celebrate San Antonio's heritage. Jane mentioned that she worked for Red Rock Readingworks, a children's literacy foundation, and asked Isabella if she would consider giving a presentation on her artistic blankets and tapestries to the children during Cultural Awareness Day. Isabella agreed, and she'd thoroughly enjoyed talking to the kids. But more than that, she and Jane had really hit it off, and their friendship had continued to blossom.

Jane reached for a tortilla chip, the diamond on her left hand sparkling. But the glimmer didn't just stop at the ring. There was a happy glow in Jane's eyes these days, which was not only sweet but ironic.

Just after Christmas, Isabella and several of her unattached friends had met at Red for dinner and margaritas. The conversation turned to men and relationships. Before the end of the evening, they'd each vowed to be married within the next twelve months. Jane, however, was the only one at the table who'd opted out of the "Single No More" pact. Now here she was, engaged to Isabella's cousin Jorge Mendoza, the one-time playboy in the family. A man who also happened to be Christina, Gloria and Sierra's brother.

"So tell me about the businessman," Christina said. "Did he have any romantic potential?"

"Not an ounce." Isabella reached for a chip. "He was in his late fifties and married. I'm beginning to think that you four have snagged all the decent men around here."

"I'm sure there's one or two left," Christina said with a smile. "The right guy will come along when you least expect it."

"I'm sure he will." Isabella returned her cousin's smile, playing the Pollyanna game even though she'd recently begun to wonder if Mr. Right would really come along. She'd gone out on a number of dates since January, but all of the men proved to be disappointments.

"Isabella, I hope you're not putting too much stock in that list you created," Jane said.

Isabella dipped a tortilla chip into the homemade salsa. "I made that list for a reason."

"Which is…?" Sierra prodded.

"To keep focused on what's really important and not fall prey to hormones and impulses. My parents fell in lust and married young. And it was a mistake from the get-go."

The young couple had divorced when Isabella was a toddler, and her mom had remarried and relocated to California, taking Isabella with her.

Gloria placed her elbows on the table and leaned

forward. "I had no idea you made a list. So, let's hear it. What are you looking for in a man?"

Isabella finished munching on the chip in her mouth before answering. "I'm looking for someone down to earth and with a steady job. Someone who's sensitive and caring and isn't afraid of commitment. A guy with a good sense of humor."

"What about his physical appearance?" Gloria asked.

Isabella winced, knowing she shouldn't be too picky, but she was. Her heritage had become so important to her that, in her heart of hearts, she knew the man she would marry would have to be Latino, too.

"Well," she said, "it would be nice if he was handsome, of course, but that's not the top priority for me."

She left it at that. It might sound old-fashioned, but she really wanted a man she could love, a man who would love her back. A man who wasn't afraid of the teamwork it would take to make a marriage last. So making a list had seemed logical, smart even. But, deep inside, she feared that she was being unrealistic, that her requirements might be too hard to fulfill.

Still, the only way to reach the stars was to aim for them. Right?

Footsteps sounded, and Isabella glanced to her right, across the fountain.

When she spotted J.R. Fortune entering the courtyard and carrying two longneck bottles of beer, she tensed. It irked her that she felt a little on edge whenever she ran into him, and today was no different.

Why couldn't he have chosen to eat indoors?

She watched him approach a table at the far corner

of the courtyard, where a man sat with his back to her. J.R. set one of the beers in front of his companion, then took a seat.

Isabella couldn't help wondering who the other man was, and in spite of her resolve to ignore them both, she stole another glance their way, just in time to see William Fortune, Sr. turn toward his eldest son.

That wasn't surprising. The two men weren't just related; they were business associates.

Her dad had told her that immediately after college, J.R. had gone to work with his father at Fortune Forecasting, a successful company that predicted marketplace trends. And before long, J.R.'s leadership skills helped him move up the corporate ladder until he was second in command behind his dad and key to the company's success.

But J.R. had given it all up recently and bought a ranch in the area. Talk about a fish out of water. J.R. might wear denim and spurs—and wear them well—but he was just a city slicker, as far as Isabella was concerned.

So far, he hadn't noticed her, which was for the best. The two of them were ill suited as a couple, even if he hadn't realized it yet.

Her luck didn't hold, though. The next time she looked his way, he flashed her a charming smile.

"Do I detect a bit of romantic interest in a certain someone?" Gloria asked.

Isabella tore her gaze from the other table and slowly shook her head. "We're just acquaintances. We met at Fiesta last year and keep running into each other. That's all."

"Forgive me for bursting your bubble," Christina said, "but that man is definitely interested in you. I've seen the way he looks at you, the way he acts when he's around you."

"Maybe a bit," Isabella admitted.

"I'd say you're interested, too," Jane added. "You've been craning your neck ever since he walked in. Not that I blame you."

Isabella's cheeks warmed at being found out, but that still didn't mean anything. "All right, let's say I'm a little attracted to him in a physical sense. Who wouldn't be? But trust me, he's not my type."

"Oh, no?" Christina asked. "He's down to earth and he's got a steady job. Sounds like a hot prospect to me."

Isabella couldn't disagree more. The man had given up a lucrative career at the age of forty in hopes of becoming a rancher. How down to earth was that? And as for a steady job, he might have plenty of money, but ranching was just a hobby for him. He'd probably grow tired of it and be back in L.A. by this time next year.

Even so, she didn't want to badmouth the man. The Fortunes and the Mendozas were close friends. And Gloria, who sat across the table from Isabella, was now a Fortune by marriage. So she tempered her response and offered them another reason a relationship with J.R. wouldn't last, even though it might sound superficial, since they might not understand all that was behind it. "My culture is very important to me, and, well, I'm focusing my search on a Latino."

Hooking up with J.R. Fortune might be a coup for

other single women in Red Rock, but in her case, it would be a disaster.

Yet in spite of her resolve to ignore J.R. completely, she couldn't help glancing back at the table where he sat with his father and wondering if her name would come up.

"You didn't need to get up and get those beers," William Fortune, Sr., said. "That waitress would have eventually come back to check on us and remember we'd ordered them."

While they'd eaten an early lunch, J.R. and his father had been discussing his plans for the ranch. But as they'd finished the last of their tacos, a Mexican beer with lime sounded good, and the waitress was nowhere to be found.

"I didn't mind getting them. Besides, I have something to celebrate." J.R. lifted an ice-cold bottle of Corona toward his dad in a toastlike motion.

His dad lifted his longneck in a similar manner. "What's that?"

"I have the deed to my new ranch in hand."

J.R. raised the bottle to his lips and savored a refreshing swallow, as his father did the same.

"By the way," J.R. said, "I've decided on a name for the property."

"Oh, yeah? What's that?"

"Molly's Pride." His voice cracked just a bit as he added, "Mom would have really loved the place."

His dad's eyes grew misty, as they often did whenever anyone brought up Molly Fortune's name. "You're right about that. But then again, she would have loved anything you set your mind to, son."

That was true.

Two years ago, Molly had passed away, leaving a hole in the family, as well as an emptiness in J.R. It wasn't as though he'd spent that much time with his mother, but he valued her opinion and her unwavering support. And she'd always been just a phone call away.

They all missed her, but of his brothers, J.R. suspected that he missed her the most.

His dad took another sip of beer. "Believe it or not, I'm considering a move to Red Rock, too."

The news came as a surprise, although J.R. wasn't sure why it did. Red Rock had been a home away from home to all of them.

"There's something about this town that has always appealed to me," William said. "And now that you, Darr and Nicholas have moved here…"

J.R. understood the draw to Red Rock. When he was a teenager, he would fly out each summer and visit his father's cousin, Ryan, and his wife, Lily, on the Double Crown Ranch. He enjoyed riding horses, listening to country music and playing cowboy for a few weeks each year.

The trips continued when he reached adulthood, although he hadn't found time to visit as often as he would have liked. Then, around his fortieth birthday, he'd begun to feel restless in Los Angeles. And that inexplicable itch grew steadily until he began to question the choices he'd made in life.

Sure, he'd succeeded in business and was well-respected in marketing circles, but he'd eventually gotten bored with the whole corporate scene and realized that there was something missing in his life. Something elusive yet very important.

"There's another reason I feel compelled to move," his dad said.

"What's that?"

"I was talking to my brother Patrick about the fires and those mysterious letters."

During the New Year's Eve party, Patrick was slipped a note that he didn't notice until later. It read, "One of the Fortunes is not who you think." William and their sister, Cindy, received similar letters, and so did Lily, their cousin Ryan's widow.

Then there were the fires, first at Red, which was later deemed arson. At the time, no one had thought the restaurant fire was related to the notes. After all, what did the two families have in common, other than friendship?

But now J.R. wasn't so sure.

After a second fire—at the Double Crown—Lily received a note that said, "This one wasn't an accident, either."

William, Sr., his blond hair now laced with silver, studied his beer, then looked up. "Someone is trying to intimidate the Fortunes, and I'm not going to stand for it. The family will be safer if we all stick together."

J.R. hoped it was just a matter of intimidation. But he understood his father's determination to present a united front.

The waitress finally returned and picked up their empty plates. "Can I get you anything else?"

"Just the check," William said.

When she left them alone again, William asked, "Are you happy you made the move to Red Rock?"

"Yes. I'm just sorry I didn't do it sooner." At the beginning of the year J.R. had come to a New Year's Eve party at Red, where they'd celebrated the Fortune Foundation's fourth year of operation. "The trip I made in January was both nostalgic and therapeutic. And the closer it got to the day of departure, the more I regretted having to return to the rat race in Los Angeles."

"I feel the same way now. I've been tossing around the idea of retiring ever since your mom died. My heart just isn't in the company anymore. I find myself valuing my family more than ever. And most of my family is now here."

"There's definitely something very appealing about the slower pace in Texas."

And for J.R., there was also a certain Latina artisan he'd met last spring, a distant relative of the Mendozas. He'd never been into long-distance relationships, so he hadn't done anything about his attraction back then.

But now that he was here?

J.R. glanced across the fountain at the table where Isabella Mendoza dined. He couldn't help watching her.

With that silky veil of long, dark hair and those big brown eyes, the artisan/interior designer was a stunningly beautiful woman.

Today she wore a turquoise blouse and a handcrafted belt in bright Southwestern shades. The colors she'd chosen to wear with a pair of black denim pants reminded him of the blankets and tapestries she wove.

He'd been intrigued by her from the first time they'd

met, and his attraction had only grown stronger. In fact, if truth be told, his interest in her had played at least a small part in his decision to move to Red Rock. And now that he was a local, he'd set his mind on asking her out.

"She's a lovely woman," William said.

J.R. turned his attention back to his father. "Excuse me?"

"Isabella. She's the one you're looking at, isn't she? The others are all taken, as far as I know."

J.R. grinned. "Yeah. She's the one."

He'd had his eye on her for quite a while and had gotten close to asking her out once, but she'd changed the subject. If he'd had any reason to believe that she didn't share his attraction and interest, he would have dropped it then and there, but he'd caught her watching him too many times to believe it was just a coincidence.

The waitress brought the bill, and J.R. reached for it, but his father snatched it first.

"Lunch is on me, son."

A few minutes later, after receiving his change and leaving a tip, William got to his feet. "Maybe you ought to stop by her table and ask her out."

But J.R. didn't need nudging.

Isabella tried to keep her mind on the conversation going on around her, but she completely lost her focus when she heard approaching footsteps.

She looked up and saw J.R. Fortune heading to their table.

Uh-oh. She sat up a bit straighter, her senses on alert.

Yet the other women turned toward him like flowers to the sun, smiled and opened right up to him.

"Well, if it isn't our newest property owner and resident," Christina said. "Welcome to Red Rock, J.R."

"Thanks," he said. "The house needs a lot of work, but as soon as I can, I'll throw a party for all my family and friends. I can't wait to show off the place."

As Sierra and Gloria added their own welcome-home/I'd-love-to-see-it speeches, Isabella kept her mouth shut. It wasn't that she was trying to be rude, but she just couldn't see J.R. as a permanent fixture in town.

He really should have stayed in Los Angeles, running the family business by day and enjoying the cultural offerings of a big city by night. Ranching was hard work—and not nearly as glamorous as he might think.

Jane pointed to the empty table beside them. "Why don't you pull up a chair and join us?"

"I don't want to interrupt your lunch." He glanced at Isabella, as though waiting for her to give him the go-ahead.

But she couldn't bring herself to do anything other than smile weakly. Sure, he'd caught her looking at him a few times today—and in the past—but never in a coy or flirtatious way. So she hoped he hadn't gotten the impression that she might want to date him.

She just found him interesting, that's all. He was a novelty of sorts, at least here in Red Rock.

Apparently, her lack of enthusiasm at Jane's invitation for him to sit with them didn't bother him in the least, because he grabbed a chair and slid it between Christina and her.

Great. She placed her hand on the menu, fingered the edges, wanting to open it, to focus on the food options, all of which she knew by heart. Instead, she couldn't help thinking about the man who'd wedged in next to her and the scent of a musky aftershave that stirred her senses.

"I can't stay long," he said, "but I have a question I'd like to ask Isabella."

Oh, no. Surely he didn't plan to ask her out in front of her friends. Well, if he did, she would just turn him down in front of them.

"I'm looking for a professional decorator."

At that revelation, she immediately gave him her undivided attention.

His gaze zeroed in on hers. "Would you be interested in giving me a proposal to redecorate the ranch house?"

The old Marshall place? The two-hundred-year-old house that had once been a hacienda? Was he kidding? Her heart spun in her chest, but she didn't dare let him see how eager she was to land the job.

"I...uh...yes," she said. "I'd be interested in drawing up a proposal."

Breathe, she told herself. She couldn't possibly let him suspect she'd be tempted to do the work for free because the exposure and the ability to add it to her professional portfolio would be a real coup.

Her mind raced as her excitement built. She'd give him a competitive price, though. And, being practical, she'd make sure she netted a small profit. The sooner she built up her bank account, the sooner she could move into a real studio and open up a storefront shop. Not that she didn't appreciate working out of the detached garage in her father's backyard, but she needed to establish herself as a professional. And having her own place was the next step in reaching that goal.

"I'm eager to get going," J.R. said. "I want to know exactly what I'm doing with the interior before I give the contractor the go-ahead to get started."

The contractor? Surely he didn't plan to let someone come in and tear out walls or make any structural changes to the building. The Marshall place was a historic landmark. What was he thinking?

Slow down, she warned herself. If he was calling in a decorator first, that meant he would respect the decorator's opinion, giving her or him a say.

She *so* had to land this job, and for a hundred different reasons. She glanced at her friends, saw them glued to the conversation she was having with J.R. They were probably making all kinds of romantic assumptions, but she wouldn't worry about that now.

Taking a breath, she said, "The Marshall house has great potential, J.R. I'm glad you've decided to get a decorator's opinion, and I'd be happy to give you mine."

"I'm sure you're busy," he said, "but do you have time to take a look at the ranch in the next couple of days?"

She *was* busy. She'd been working hard to get ready for this year's Fiesta. Opening day was on the sixteenth and would be here before she knew it. But this job—or rather this potential job—was too important to pass up, so she would make the time.

"What day did you have in mind?" she asked.

"Like I said, I want to get started right away. The kitchen needs to be modernized. My poor housekeeper is doing the best she can under the circumstances, but the appliances have to be replaced. And I don't want to do this in a piecemeal fashion."

The thought of modernizing that old hacienda tied Isabella's stomach in a knot. There were ways to update and make it functional without losing its historic value. But would someone like J.R. go for it?

Hopefully, if she were awarded the job, he would give her free rein.

With every beat of her heart, her confidence grew.

This project, which had at first seemed to be the epitome of a professional challenge, as well as a financial blessing, had taken on an even greater importance. She felt something stir inside her.

Getting involved in refurbishing J.R.'s house would give her an opportunity to preserve Texas history. It was the perfect project for her. And she was the perfect choice—if she could only convince J.R.

"Would tomorrow work for you?" she asked.

"That would be great." His eyes sparked with obvious pleasure, and his smile caused a single dimple to form in his cheek.

For the briefest of moments, she wondered if there might be just a bit more to his enthusiasm than landing a decorator, but she shrugged it off. She was a professional who knew how to keep things on a business level.

"Is nine o'clock too early?" he asked.

She would have agreed to a six o'clock start if it wouldn't have made her sound too eager. "That's fine. I'll see you at nine."

"Good. I hope you'll block off most of the day. It's

going to be a big job—and a costly one. But I have some ideas I'd like to talk over with you, and I want to make sure it's done right."

So much for having free rein.

Still, Isabella would give it her best shot. She needed the job—and she really wanted it.

Even if it meant bumping heads with J.R. Fortune every step of the way.

Chapter Two

The next day, Isabella arrived at J.R.'s ranch at a quarter to nine. Since the old hacienda was located about ten miles from downtown Red Rock, and she wasn't exactly sure how long it would take to get there from her father's house in San Antonio, she'd left earlier than she'd needed to.

As she drove her little red pickup along the graveled drive, kicking up dust, the property was abuzz with activity. Several ranch hands were repairing a stretch of fence along the way, and, next to the barn, a carpenter was busy working with a skill saw and a stack of lumber.

J.R. hadn't been kidding. He *was* eager to whip this property into shape.

And speaking of the new rancher, there he was, talking to a tall, lanky man wearing a leather toolbelt.

In a pair of faded denim jeans, J.R. appeared to fit

right in with both the hands and the construction crew, but his new Stetson and boots shouted, "city slicker."

He glanced up when he heard her pickup approach and grinned, yet he continued to direct the workers.

J.R. may not know much about ranching, but he was definitely a take-charge type, which wasn't surprising. Those white-collar execs usually were.

Still, he was a handsome man, even though he had to be completely out of his league with this sort of thing. But she wouldn't let that slow her down. She was here to study the house, take measurements, sketch out a rough draft of the floor plan and the layout of the outbuildings. All the while, she would let her imagination take flight.

Everything else was secondary.

She slipped out of the driver's seat, reached for both her purse and her briefcase, then stepped out of the vehicle. Normally, she preferred to wear heels whenever possible, but since she had no idea what she'd be getting into today, she'd chosen a pair of moccasin-style boots.

J.R. lifted a finger, indicating he'd be just a minute. She nodded then brushed a hand along the crinkled fabric of her colorful, Southwestern-style skirt, which she'd accessorized with handcrafted silver and turquoise jewelry.

She usually wore her long hair loose, but since it sometimes got in the way when she worked, she'd woven it into a single braid that hung down her back.

As she waited for J.R. to finish instructing the foreman, she studied the exterior of the hacienda, its adobe brick showing under aged, white stucco.

A baroque stone entrance with a Moorish-style arch

led to a solid wooden door, which had to be more than a century old—maybe two—and was remarkable in more ways than one.

The yard, she realized, as she turned to take it all in, would need a gardener. With a good pruning and some tasteful landscaping, the trees and plants would add tremendously to the exterior.

J.R. had been right: the place needed a lot of work. But Isabella couldn't still a burst of excitement at the chance to take part in refurbishing the hacienda.

"I'm sorry to keep you waiting," J.R. said, as he joined her.

She turned and smiled. "It's beautiful."

"I think so, too." He motioned toward the door. "Come on in. I'll show you the interior."

He followed her through the archway that led to the entrance. She opened the door, and they entered. The years, it seemed, rolled back, providing a glimpse of days gone by, of Dons and rancheros, of vaqueros and señoritas.

For the most part, the house was empty, which allowed her to focus on the white plaster walls, the wood-beam ceilings and the distressed-wood floors.

"What do you think?" he asked.

She turned, trying her best to curb her awe and enthusiasm and probably failing. "It's…amazing."

The distinctive structure and layout had great potential, and she again thought of the many positive repercussions of landing the job.

"You're the expert," he said. "What do you think about Spanish tile floors?"

Her jaw dropped, and her eyes opened wide. "Oh, no. This wood needs to stay. Some people pay an arm and a leg to re-create what you already have. All this floor needs is a little polish."

"I was talking about expensive tile, something hand-crafted and imported."

"I'm sure it would be lovely," she said. "*In another home.* Not this one. The original wood flooring needs to stay."

He paused a beat, as though not sure how to handle their first disagreement. Then a slow grin stretched across his face. Flecks of gold glimmered in his hazel irises, turning her heart on edge, and she forced herself to focus on the open space surrounding them and the high-beamed ceilings and thick stone walls. The only furniture in sight was a leather recliner and a side table that sported a hardcover novel and a lamp.

The absence of any of the usual comforts had made her assume he was living elsewhere. But that book and the lamp...

"Where are you staying?" she asked.

"Right here. I found some old furniture in one of the outbuildings, and I brought a few pieces inside. I have a bed and a chest of drawers in the master bedroom. I didn't want to get too carried away until I brought in a decorator."

"If you don't mind," she said, "I'd like to see what else is in that outbuilding. I'd also like to be free to wander the grounds, to make notes and do a few sketches. I won't get in the way of the workers."

"Of course." He placed his hand on her back in a

polite, gracious manner, but his touch sent a rush of heat through her bloodstream.

What was with that?

She shook off the physical reaction as well as she could and allowed him to guide her through an arched doorway.

"I want to introduce you to my housekeeper and cook," he said. "If you need anything, she should be able to help or to answer any questions you might have."

J.R.'s hand slowly dropped, and she missed the contact instantly, even though her skin and spine still hummed from his touch.

She continued through the walkway until she reached the kitchen, where she was met with the aroma of chili and spice. No doubt, it came from whatever was inside a shiny copper kettle simmering on top of the stove, a big, bulky model from the late fifties and early sixties. The white appliance had been cleaned to a glossy shine, its chrome trim sparkling.

A sixty-something woman with salt-and-pepper hair stood at the sink, rinsing vegetables. She turned toward the doorway when Isabella and J.R. entered the room.

"Evie," he said, "I want to introduce you to Isabella Mendoza. She's the decorator I spoke to you about."

Evie, her cheeks plump with a natural blush, smiled. "How do you do?"

"Fine, thank you." Isabella returned her smile. "Something sure smells good."

The matronly woman beamed. "Thank you. I'm making sauce for the chicken."

Isabella took a quick scan of the kitchen, noting that it would need a lot of work to make it more functional, then returned her gaze to the woman who appeared to be doing the best with what she had.

"I'm going to be wandering around the house for a while," Isabella said. "I'll try not to get underfoot."

"Don't worry about that," Evie replied. "I'll be glad to step aside. Mr. Fortune said he wouldn't make any big changes until he'd had a chance to work with the decorator, and my job will be a lot easier once this kitchen is modernized."

"Evie," J.R. said, "I meant to tell you earlier that there would be two for lunch."

"I'll set up a table in the courtyard, unless, of course, you'd like to eat in the office."

"The courtyard might be a nice change." J.R. turned to Isabella and smiled. "Until I purchase a dining set, I've been eating at my desk."

"Every meal?" she asked.

He shrugged. "I've gotten used to working through quite a few meals. Come on, I'll show you the office. I've got the computer set up with an Internet connection. There's also an adding machine, a copier and a fax. You can use whatever you need."

As J.R. led her out of the kitchen and down a hallway, she said, "You've certainly been busy. You've got a crew started on the fencing and repairing the barn. And you've even hired a cook."

"I *have* been busy, but Evie has worked for me for years. When I left Los Angeles, I asked her to come to Texas and help me set up my household."

"She sounds loyal."

"Yes, she is. If her husband hadn't passed away las

year, she wouldn't have made the move with me. But her only family is a couple of stepkids who are closer to their mother than they are to her. I suppose that's only natural, but Evie practically raised them."

"That's too bad," she said.

"I know. Family is important."

Yes, but family dynamics could be very complicated, especially when it came to a yours-mine-and-ours situation. Isabella knew that firsthand.

She'd been raised in California by her Anglo stepdad, and while she'd been treated well and cared for, she'd always felt a bit out of place and out of step. And once her stepfather remarried and started a new family, that feeling of being on the outside looking in had only gotten worse.

But there'd been a happy ending.

Five years ago, when she was finally reunited with her biological father in Red Rock, the entire Mendoza clan had welcomed her with open arms. As a result, she wholeheartedly embraced the Mendozas and the Tejana culture of her roots.

As J.R. led her back to the room he was using as an office, she glanced through a few open doorways, only to see empty rooms with the same plastered walls and wood ceilings. Each room, it seemed, had a fireplace. Wood-burning, she assumed.

"The office is on the left," J.R. said.

Isabella stepped inside, then took a seat across from him at a massive mahogany desk. She scanned the rustic room, which had been decorated with a desk, a bookshelf and modern-style wooden file cabinets.

While obviously expensive and of high quality, the furniture just didn't fit the house.

"I hope you plan on keeping the place much the same as it was," she said.

"To an extent. The contractor said the structure is sound, so I don't see a need to make any major changes."

Before she could respond, a little growl sounded, and she felt a tug on her boot.

"Hey." She glanced down to see a roly-poly Australian shepherd puppy chewing on the leather fringe and bent to pick up the little guy. "Aren't you the cutest little thing. Where did you come from?"

"Sorry about that," J.R. said. "That's Baron, my future cattle dog. Right now, he's kind of a pest."

"He's so sweet."

As if knowing that he'd scored a hit and made a new friend, Baron licked her face.

The only trouble was, when Isabella glanced at J.R. and saw a grin stretch across his face, she got the feeling that he thought he'd scored one, too.

At a quarter to twelve, J.R. headed to the washroom in the barn to clean up for lunch. He was eager to talk to Isabella, to see what kind of plan she'd come up with.

He'd told her that he was soliciting bids and proposals from several decorators, and he certainly could. But what she didn't know was that the job was hers if she wanted it. He would just make sure that it was in the contract that she would have to get his okay on anything major.

After washing up, he headed for the house. Once

inside, he stopped by the kitchen, where Evie was getting ready to serve lunch.

"Have you seen Isabella?" he asked.

"She was in here a few minutes ago, taking measurements and making a sketch. And I have to admit, I'm glad she's here."

Oh, yeah? "Why's that?"

"Because the rascally pup has decided to follow her around rather than tagging along after me and getting under my feet." Evie feigned a scoff, which J.R. knew better than to take seriously. That pup had both of them wrapped around his little paw.

"Can I do anything to help?" he asked.

"No. I've got the table set on the patio. Lunch will be served as soon as you're ready."

"Thanks, Evie."

J.R. went in search of Isabella, finding her in the alcove that led to the courtyard. Baron was sitting a few steps away, scratching his ear.

She had her head bent over a yellow tablet as she made notes to herself. She'd braided her hair today, which was too bad. J.R. liked it better when she wore it long and sleek. A man could fantasize about hair like that.

Actually, he had.

"How's it going?" he asked.

She glanced up and grinned, her dark eyes dancing with ideas and possibilities. "Great."

"Are you ready for a lunch break?"

"I am, if you are." She lowered the notepad to her side. "Each time I've walked near the kitchen, I've taken a whiff of whatever Evie is making. Now I'm starving."

"Evie's the best cook I've ever had." J.R. motioned toward the archway that led to the courtyard. "After you."

She glanced at the puppy. "Come on, Baron. You followed me to every nook and cranny of this big old house. Don't poop out on me now."

The puppy perked up, then trotted along beside her.

J.R. couldn't blame the little guy. He found himself lured by her, too. And as he fell into step behind her, he couldn't keep his eyes off the sway of her hips, the swish of her colorful skirt.

Isabella had an eye for color and style, which had been another thing that had intrigued him since day one.

The courtyard had been swept clean, but it was still a far cry from what it had once been, from what it would someday be again.

Evie had covered the old, glass-topped table with a linen cloth. A vase with several wild roses, which had come from the scraggly bushes near the entrance to the house, added a splash of pink.

"Isn't this a great place to eat?" Isabella asked, as she took in the table, as well as her rustic surroundings.

Someday, it would be, J.R. thought. "It's going to take some work."

"Yes, I know, but in my mind, I can see the finished product." She lifted her hand and flicked her wrist in a would-you-just-look-at-this manner. "Imagine it filled with lush hanging plants, as well as clay pots of bougainvillea."

He envied her imagination, since he couldn't quite get past all the time, work and money that it would take.

"I figure one of the first things that needs to be done is to tear out and replace the fountain."

"I don't think so." She stepped closer to the stone fountain, the gold and orange tile chipped and cracked. "The plumbing needs to be completely replaced, and it will have to be retiled. But this looks like it might be the original, and I'd hate to see it lost."

J.R. held out a wrought-iron chair for Isabella and waited until she took a seat. Then he sat across from her.

Moments later, Evie brought in a tray with two salad plates filled with fresh greens and red and yellow grape tomatoes. Each was topped with a dollop of homemade guacamole dressing and sprinkled with grated cojita cheese.

"Thanks, Evie."

She grinned. "You're welcome." Then she returned to the kitchen.

"What did you think of the rest of the house?" J.R. asked.

"It's fabulous. The artist in me is impressed with the quality of the structure, with the potential. And I hope you'll allow me to be your decorator."

Something told him not to be too easy, too agreeable. It would be best if she didn't suspect he had a game plan at work here. But he didn't want to string her along, either. "The Fortunes and the Mendozas have been friends for a long time, so you've definitely got the edge over anyone else, Isabella. As long as your price isn't outrageous and we have the same vision for the place, I don't see a problem."

She glanced around the sparse, run-down courtyard,

at the fountain that was dry and dusty from age and lack of use. "This was meant to be the center of the home, so it should be the center of the decor."

"Are you suggesting we start here? With the fountain?"

"Yes." She placed her elbows on the table and leaned forward. "I know a Mexican craftsman in San Antonio who would do a wonderful job. He's the one who refurbished the fountain at Red."

"That sounds good to me."

"This place could be a showcase."

He hoped so, although he wasn't interested in impressing anyone. He just wanted his house to be all that it was meant to be. To him, that was important. "I don't know if I told you this or not, but I'm calling the ranch Molly's Pride. After my mother."

"I didn't know her," Isabella said. "But I've heard she was a wonderful woman."

"She was." The eldest of five boys, J.R. had grown up in a loving but rambunctious home. The entire family was incredibly close, but J.R. had shared a special bond with his mom. "My mother was just as comfortable in a formal dining room as she was in a fort my brothers and I built in the backyard."

"It sounds like she was the kind of mom who didn't just love her kids, she enjoyed them, too."

"Yes, she did. She was our biggest champion, but she wasn't a pushover. She made each of us toe the line."

"From what I heard, she had a lot to cheer about when it came to her firstborn."

J.R. had always taken his achievements in stride, and

to hear Isabella mention them, to see her eyeing him with an appreciative grin—or was it merely a polite one?—made him feel a bit…awkward.

Fortunately, Evie chose that time to remove their salads and to replace them with plates bearing grilled chicken with a light covering of spicy tomato sauce, steamed broccoli and rice.

After J.R. and Isabella both thanked her, she slipped back into the kitchen, leaving them alone.

J.R.'s curiosity finally got the better of him. "So what else did you hear about me?"

"That you were the typical eldest son—an overachiever who excelled in school, that you were a star athlete in football and baseball. That you were social and always on the go."

He shrugged, that sense of awkwardness building and shoving him back in his seat.

Was she talking about him dating a lot? Was she trolling for details?

Or was she just making polite conversation?

It was hard to say, but, either way, he didn't kiss and tell. The truth was that he'd had his share of relationships over the years, but nothing serious.

Maybe because, deep inside, he'd been looking for someone like his mom to round out his life and to be the mother of his children. A few of the women he'd dated had come close, but he'd always found them lacking.

He couldn't put his finger on just what he was looking for, but he had a feeling he'd know it when he saw it.

Not that he was looking all that hard. Life was good, and he was happy.

For the most part, anyway.

"To be honest," she said, "I was really surprised to hear that you'd given up your career in Los Angeles and moved to Red Rock."

"Why?"

She took a sip of her water. "This seems like such an abrupt change for such a successful businessman."

"The decision wasn't made lightly."

Four months ago, on New Year's Eve, J.R. returned to Red Rock for a gathering at Red. Emmett Jamison had rented out the entire restaurant for a benefit to celebrate a banner year for the Fortune Foundation, an organization founded in Ryan Fortune's memory. When it was time for J.R. to fly home, he'd wanted to extend his trip, but hadn't been able to.

Then, in February, Patrick Fortune called a family council meeting at the Double Crown to discuss the mysterious letters he and some of the others had received. While in town, J.R. had given in to the urge, called a realtor and begun scouting for parcels. But the only properties that appealed to him were ranches.

Again he went back to L.A., but his heart and his mind were still in Texas.

Next came the fires, the first one at Red and the second at the Double Crown. When arson was suspected, the Fortunes and the Mendozas began to circle the wagons, and J.R. felt drawn to Red Rock more than ever. Two of his brothers were living there now, and he decided it was time to join them.

The realtor kept e-mailing listings to him, and he'd spent a lot of time doing research on the Internet.

One ranch in particular struck his fancy, and he felt compelled to place an offer on it, knowing that a purchase like that would change his entire life. Yet instead of being unsettling, the idea of moving to Texas was energizing. And he couldn't think of a good reason not to follow through on it.

He could be having a midlife crisis, he supposed. And maybe he was reacting to his mother's death. But the reasons didn't seem to matter. Like many of the Fortune men, he was used to doing and getting whatever he wanted.

So, when his offer was accepted, he gave up his position at Fortune Forecasting and moved to Red Rock. It was as simple as that. And even if others might not understand his decision, it had been right for him.

"Are you happy?" she asked, interrupting his thoughts—or maybe picking up on them.

Happy? He'd never given that much thought. He'd always sought contentment in life. Success, peace of mind.

"Are you asking whether I like the rural life?"

"Yes, I suppose I am."

"I definitely love being here. It's all pretty new to me, but I'm a quick study. And I'm surrounding myself with others who have the experience I lack. I've already hired a foreman and several ranch hands, and I've started buying cattle." It all felt *good. Right.*

But if he was perfectly honest with himself, he wasn't what you'd call happy. There was still something missing in his life.

As he glanced across the table at the pretty Tejana artisan, as he watched her close her eyes and savor the taste of her meal in a way that made him hungry for a lot more than lunch, he knew just what it was.

Once at home, Isabella sat at her kitchen table and immediately began working on her vision for J.R.'s home. She pulled out some catalogues and did some online research, too.

It was after midnight when she finally shut down the computer and went to bed, but she was up again at dawn, eager to draw up a proposal J.R. couldn't refuse.

Just after two o'clock in the afternoon, she finally put the finishing touches on her bid, at which time she faxed it to him. Since he was probably outside, overseeing the ranch hands and the construction crew, she had no idea how long it would take for him to even notice the pages in his fax machine, let alone get back to her. So she focused on the pressing job at hand: preparing her blankets and tapestries for this year's Fiesta.

When she first moved to San Antonio, her dad's offer to let her use his garage had been everything she'd been looking for and the answer to a prayer. It might not have been quite as roomy as she would have liked, but rent-free was certainly what she'd call affordable.

In the back of the garage, near the bathroom, she'd created an office area. She'd set up a workshop in the center, and in front, close to the entrance, she'd created a Peg-Board display area for her work.

But as her business grew and her reputation spread, she'd gradually outgrown the garage.

Now, as she went through her tapestries, choosing

the ones to take to the Fiesta next week, her excitement built. April was going to be a busy month. In addition to the ten-day Fiesta, which began on the sixteenth, and a possible job decorating J.R.'s hacienda, her birthday was on the twenty-third.

This year, she'd be turning thirty. Some people struggled when they entered a new decade of life, and Isabella had to admit that it niggled at her a bit. Actually, if she wasn't still single, it probably wouldn't bother her at all.

The door at the studio entrance opened, and the bell her dad had installed for her tinkled, alerting her to either a client, a customer or a visitor.

"I'll be right there." She left the fringe trim she'd been stitching on the worktable, then made her way to the front door.

With her studio in her father's backyard, she didn't have as many customers as she would get if she had a storefront shop. But that time would come.

As she stepped around the paneled Peg-Board that doubled as a barrier separating the front of the workshop from the back, her heart dropped to her stomach when she spotted J.R. standing with his hat in hand, looking far more handsome and appealing than he should.

Her heart jumped and thumped at the sight of him, a teenage, crushlike reaction that made absolutely no sense at all.

"What a surprise," she said, downplaying her wacky pulse rate and willing it to slow down.

"Your fax came through about an hour ago," he said. "After looking it over, I decided to drive out and talk to you."

He could have phoned, but she decided not to point that out.

So why was he here? Had she made an error in the math? Had she projected a cost that he thought was too high?

Too low?

Had he come to negotiate or barter?

She wanted the job badly, so she'd cut the price as much as she could without selling herself and her talent short. Her numbers were competitive already.

"I told you I was eager to get started," he said, "so I wanted to discuss the bid, as well as throw out another idea I had. And if we can reach an agreement this afternoon, I'm prepared to write a check for the deposit."

Wait. What about the other bids? Did he already have some in hand to compare hers to?

She ran her palms along her black denim-clad hips, hiding any trace of moisture that might have gathered. "Why don't you follow me back to my office. We can go over the proposal and the figures."

"All right."

As she led him around the partition, she asked, "Which item concerned you?"

"Overall, I liked your ideas and suggestions. So this is really just a request."

Once at her desk, she pulled up a stool for him. Instead of taking her own seat, she reached for the backrest of the office chair and remained standing, her fingers clutching the faux leather.

He chose to stand, too, which made him appear much taller than she'd remembered. More commanding, more vibrant. He wore a boyish, kiss-the-girls-and-make-them-squirm grin, which made her feel a lot younger than she'd felt just minutes ago.

Maybe she ought to sit down after all.

As she took a seat, he did, too.

"The price is more than fair for all the work you'll be doing," he said.

Why did she expect him to throw in a big "*But...*"?

Or to suggest that they paint the interior some hideous combination of colors?

When he did neither, curiosity got the better of her and she quizzed him. "What's on your mind?"

"For the most part, I like your vision for the place. So the job is yours."

A flood of relief, mingled with pleasure, washed over her. Decorating Molly's Pride would keep her busy for several months. "Is that why you came by? To sign the proposal and to make a deposit?"

"In part, yes. But this is a big job, and it's important to me. I want to make sure it's done right."

Isabella had worked for fussy clients before, but for some reason, she hadn't expected J.R. to be all that particular. "I'm very conscientious. And I can provide references if you'd like them."

"No, that's not necessary."

Feeling way too much like a kid who'd been sent to the principal's office for something she hadn't done, Isabella sat up straight and tossed a long strand of hair behind her shoulder, preparing herself for whatever might be standing in the way of her getting the job.

"I have the feeling that you're going to want to take

a hands-on approach to the decorating," he said, easing into his concern.

He was right. The renovation of a historic building needed to be taken seriously, so she nodded her agreement.

"And for that reason, I hope you'll agree to my request before we lock in too many specifics in the contract."

Feeling more confused than ever, she didn't know if she should lower her guard or raise it higher. "What is it?"

"I'd like you to spend a week at the hacienda."

As she stared at J.R.'s dancing eyes, her tummy zinged and pinged in all kinds of strange ways that had nothing to do with landing the job or even the prospect of adding it to her portfolio, and everything to do with her spending time with J.R. Fortune.

Well, not *with* him, but… "I'm not sure I understand what you're asking."

"I'll give you a five-thousand dollar deposit—non-refundable. But before we sign the actual contract and you jump right into making any major changes, I'd like you to get a real feel for the house and the ranch. That's the reason I suggested we eat lunch in the courtyard yesterday. I wanted you to see it from a guest's perspective. And I'd hoped that you would see all that it was lacking, all that it could be."

That's exactly what she'd done. In her mind's eye, the imaginary plants had begun to grow and unfurl, the flowers had blossomed. She'd almost been able to hear the water gurgling in the refurbished fountain.

"If you actually stayed at the ranch and slept in one of the guestrooms, if you sat near the window in the great room and read a book, I think your work would take on a new dimension."

He had a point, she supposed. But this was the worst possible time for her to leave the studio. "I'm really busy right now, trying to get ready for Fiesta."

"I'd pay extra if you'd hire someone to do that for you."

The man definitely didn't like to take "no" for an answer. "It's not that easy, J.R. I might be able to find someone to watch the studio, but I'm the only one who can finish the last tapestries. I'd have to bring them with me and work on them at your ranch."

"That's all right with me." He flashed her a charming, boyish grin—the kind that made the girls squeal and run, yet secretly want to get caught.

As his gaze strummed over her, sending her mind scurrying to make sense of it all, she couldn't help wondering if he had ulterior motives.

If so, she ought to be leery. So what was with the buzz of excitement?

"I'd like you to immerse yourself in the history that permeates the walls," he added. "There's something special about the place. I think you've felt it, too."

She had. And it surprised her that he'd recognized that the people who'd once filled the hacienda had left something of themselves behind. Not in a ghostlike sense, but with an essence of love and joy.

Of heartache, too, she suspected.

"I think it's important for the decorator to be someone who appreciates the history behind the hacienda, as well as the culture of the people who built it with their blood, sweat and tears."

Isabella couldn't agree more. So how could she say no to that?

"All right," she said. "I'll see you on Friday afternoon."

"Good." He flashed her another charming grin, one that made her senses scatter all over again.

Chapter Three

Isabella arrived at J.R.'s ranch on Friday afternoon, the back of her sporty red pickup filled with her loom, her tapestries and her suitcase. She'd deposited his check yesterday, which made this adventure feel more like the business deal that it was.

As the vehicle kicked up dust along the driveway, she noticed that the fencing had not only been repaired, but had been painted white. And the work on the barn had progressed to the point that it no longer looked like the same weathered structure anymore.

J.R. hadn't been kidding. He was definitely intent on getting things done quickly.

She parked beside J.R.'s Escalade and reached for both her purse and her briefcase before sliding out of the driver's seat. She'd just locked the door when she heard him approach, so she turned to greet him.

As he drew closer, a warm smile crinkled the edges of his eyes, indicating he was happy to see her.

Or was that just her imagination?

"How was the drive out here?"

"Not too bad." She returned his smile, and couldn't help running her gaze over him.

He wore a pair of faded jeans and a white button-down shirt, the cuffs rolled up at the forearms. His hair was damp, as though he'd just showered.

For her? she wondered.

Oh, for Pete's sake. Where had *that* renegade thought come from? J.R. had been working all day, and it was nearing dinner time. Of course he would come out of the house fresh and clean.

"You're just in time. Evie is preparing appetizers and cocktails, which should be ready soon."

Too busy to even think about eating, Isabella had spent the morning packing up her things and the afternoon providing Sarah, the young neighbor who had agreed to look after her studio with a list of instructions. "That sounds good."

J.R. peered into the back of her pickup, then reached for her suitcase. "I'll have one of the men carry the rest of your things inside. Come with me. I'll show you to your room."

She followed him into the house, catching the clean, musky scent of both soap and aftershave.

Even if she could get past the point that he bore absolutely no resemblance to the kind of man she was looking for—she *couldn't* get involved with him. He was a client, she reminded herself. She had a job to do, and staying here was merely part of a business arrangement. Nothing more.

He led her through the house to one of the guestrooms.

Other than an antique bed that was covered with a white goose-down comforter and matching pillows, the room was fairly sparse. An etched-glass vase of pink roses—those same wild ones that had graced their lunch table the other day—sat on the chest of drawers.

The flowers were a nice touch, and she wondered who'd thought about placing them there—J.R. or Evie. She supposed it really didn't matter.

She scanned the room, thinking that it could use a fresh coat of paint, that one of her tapestries might look good on the east wall.

"This is the largest guestroom," J.R. said. "I'm not sure how much space your loom will take up, but you can set it up in a separate room, if you'd like."

He seemed to have thought of everything, and she couldn't help feeling welcome. "Thank you. It might be best if I use two rooms."

Matching nightstands, both antiques, flanked the bed. There was a gardenia-scented candle on one. The other was empty.

"I like this bedroom set," she said. "We'll need to purchase more. Where did you find it?"

"Actually, it was one of the pieces in that outbuilding I told you about. Once you settle in, I can take you there."

She couldn't imagine what other treasures were still on the ranch, just waiting to be discovered. "I'll leave the suitcase on the bed and unpack later. Let's take a look now."

J.R. grinned. "I had a feeling you'd say that. Some of that stuff needs to be hauled to the dump, but there are a few interesting antiques stored in there."

Moments later, Isabella and J.R. strode across the ranch to a set of buildings near the barn.

The sprinklers had been turned on in the pasture. She tried to picture the ranch up and running again, the cattle in the fields, the cowboys hard at work.

J.R. slowed in front of a shabby-looking building. "This is the one." He swung open the door and flipped on a light.

As Isabella stepped inside, she was assailed by the dusty scent of neglect and of years gone by.

She studied the interior, noting an old rocking chair with a broken slat in the backrest, and realized that J.R. had been right. A few of the pieces of furniture weren't usable, while others were just plain old and out of date. Still, there were some lovely antiques, including a dining room set and an armoire.

Against the far wall, she noticed a large canvas draped across a table. "What's over there?"

"Some old paintings. I have no idea whether they have any value."

Isabella wasn't an appraiser by any means, but she wanted to see the artwork for herself and determine whether they'd work as part of the décor.

As she studied each piece, checking out the frames, as well as the paintings themselves, she realized that she could use most of them—in one way or another.

"Why do you suppose all this stuff was packed away?" she asked.

"After Mr. Marshall passed away, his heirs took a few pieces with them. They were going to get rid of the rest, so I told them to leave behind anything they didn't want."

"Well, you certainly scored." She glanced over her shoulder to offer him a smile, only to see that he was standing back, watching her. She suspected that he'd been appraising her, instead of the furniture, although she couldn't be sure.

Again, she wondered if he had something up his sleeve, but she'd be darned if she could read minds.

Of course, when it came to J.R. Fortune, maybe it was just as well that she couldn't.

It was nearly five-thirty when J.R. walked Isabella back to the house. Her clothing was usually both colorful and striking, yet today she'd dressed casually. He'd never seen her in well-worn, comfortable blue jeans before, and they molded her hips every bit as nicely as he would have guessed. Still, true to form, she wore a bright red blouse and silver hoop earrings, adorned with an array of matching beads. Her hair hung in a glossy sheet down her back.

As they continued through the archway into the house, he caught a hint of her perfume—or maybe it was body lotion. He wasn't sure, but the scent, something both floral and exotic, suited her.

Their shoes clicked on the distressed-wood flooring Isabella had insisted should stay. J.R. couldn't see the beauty in it, though. He preferred Mexican tile and suspected they might bump heads over the décor as time wore on. But the important thing was that Isabella was here—close to him and immersed in beautifying the house he loved.

In the great room, Evie had placed a bottle of his favorite Napa Valley chardonnay on ice and left two crystal goblets on an old chest that served as a make-shift coffee table.

Near the hearth, where a slow and steady fire licked the logs and cast a romantic glow, Baron was curled up on his little mat, sound asleep.

Isabella crossed her arms, causing the red cotton fabric to stretch across her breasts and create a slight gap at the buttons. A pretty smile adorned her face. "Will you look at that little guy? He's snoozing as though he doesn't have a care in the world."

J.R. chuckled. "That's because I let him follow me around the ranch today, and now he's completely wiped out."

"How did he do?" she asked. "He's still pretty young."

"He chased a few butterflies, but I'm afraid he's got a lot to learn." J.R. nodded toward the crystal goblets. "Can I get you a glass of wine?"

"Yes, please."

As he poured the chardonnay, Evie entered the room long enough to drop off a plate of crackers, cheese and several small clusters of red and green grapes, as well as a hot artichoke dip.

J.R. thanked Evie, then turned to Isabella. He watched her from behind as she strode toward the fireplace, hips swaying sensually.

He'd been asking various people about her—casually, of course, so that no one would realize just how interested he was. The one who'd given him the biggest insight had been José Mendoza, her father's cousin. José and his wife, Maria, owned Red.

"I heard that you grew up in California, too," he said, as he closed the gap between them. "My family home was in Malibu. Where was yours?"

"Sacramento, Oakland, Santa Barbara. We moved around a lot, at least until I was a teenager. I went to high school in the San Diego area."

"What brought you back to Texas?"

"I'd lost touch with my real dad, so when I finally located him, he invited me to fly out to San Antonio and visit. The Mendozas welcomed me with open arms, and two days after I arrived, I knew that Texas was my home, and that I would never move again."

From what J.R. had gathered, Isabella and her father were very close. So it seemed odd that the man hadn't kept in better touch with her when she was younger. And that she wasn't resentful that he hadn't been in the picture.

"Were there hard feelings between your parents?" he asked.

"I'm not sure of the details. My mom passed away when I was eleven." She reached for a cracker, but didn't take a bite. "My father told me that, in spite of the fiery arguments he and my mom used to have, he loved her—and he adored me. He was heartbroken by the breakup, and when my mom met another man—an Anglo—and moved to California, taking me with her, he was devastated."

"Is that what he told you?"

"Yes. I also found an old letter he'd written to her, and it was very clear that he was really torn up about the divorce."

"Didn't he come to visit you?"

"He would have. I'm sure of it. But while my stepfather was good to me, he was a jealous man and didn't want my mom to remain in contact with my dad or his family. He begged my mom to let him adopt me. She actually approached my dad about it, but Dad told her absolutely not. He loved me and refused to sign over his paternal rights."

J.R. could understand that. If he had a kid, he would be a major part of that child's life.

She took a sip of her wine. "We moved around a lot in the early years. I was young and didn't think anything of it. But in retrospect, I think my stepfather might have done that on purpose so my dad couldn't find us. But I guess I'll never know for sure."

Either way, J.R. concluded, Luis Mendoza had lost touch with his daughter and was obviously glad to have her back in his life.

"When my mom died," Isabella said, "I was devastated. My stepfather took it hard, too, but it didn't take him long to find another woman. An Anglo, like him."

"You say 'Anglo' like it's a bad thing."

"I'm not the least bit prejudiced, if that's what you're thinking. But as much as my stepfather loved my mom, he didn't appreciate her heritage and banished any traces of Tejana culture from our house. He even insisted that she convert to his faith."

The guy sounded both insensitive and controlling, but J.R. kept his thoughts to himself.

"Spanish was my first language," Isabella added. "My parents were both bilingual and wanted me to be, too. They knew I'd learn English once I went to pre-school, so that had been their plan. But my stepfather discouraged my mom from speaking Spanish to me at home, and I soon forgot what little I'd learned. Even when I was in high school and needed to take a foreign language, he told me to take French."

"That's too bad."

She took another sip of wine. "Actually, my stepfather was good to me. And after he remarried, so was his wife. Yet I felt like an outsider. When my sisters were born, the entire family was fair-skinned and blue-eyed. So people naturally thought I was the neighbor or the sitter. And whenever we took family photos, I always stood out."

J.R. wanted to tell her that she'd stand out in every photograph—not because of her olive complexion, however. It was her beauty that prompted a double take. But he didn't want to risk showing his hand too soon.

"Don't get me wrong," she said. "I keep in touch with my stepparents. And we all get along much better now. But there's a distance between us, and I'm not just talking about the miles."

"How did you finally hook up with your dad?"

"After feeling especially sad one day, I went through some of my mom's belongings and found that old letter I mentioned, the one my dad had written years ago. There was a return address, and I contacted him."

"Your father must have been glad to hear from you."

"He'd been looking for me for years, so he was

ecstatic." Isabella smiled, and J.R. wondered if she'd ever looked prettier. "I was happy, too. For the first time since losing my mom, I felt loved. *Truly* loved. My father offered me airfare to fly to San Antonio, and I took it. And I'm *so* glad I did. I gained an instant family and felt as though I'd finally come home."

J.R. wondered if that was when she'd taken such a big interest in her heritage. "Thank goodness you went through that box and found that letter."

"You can say that again." She slid him another smile, one that warmed his heart from the inside out.

He lifted his half-empty glass in a toast. "Here's to finding your way back home. And to helping me decorate Molly's Pride."

As the tapping crystal resonated in the room, J.R. couldn't help but feel a growing sense of satisfaction for a job well done. He'd always known how to orchestrate things, to get people to do what he wanted them to without them being any the wiser. And that's what he'd done when he asked Isabella to give him a proposal to decorate his home.

He'd heard something about a bet she'd made with her single friends, a vow to be married before the end of next year. So he'd decided to step up his plan to get to know her better.

Since he was going to be incredibly busy over the next few months and would be virtually ranch-bound, he hadn't wanted to run the risk of some other guy sweeping Isabella off her feet before he had a chance to ask her out. So he'd made up his mind not to leave anything to chance. Isabella was too pretty, too tempting to remain unattached for very long, especially if she was actively looking for a man.

If that were the case, and if she proved to be the woman he thought she was, he'd come to an easy conclusion.

That man may as well be him.

It *had* to be the wine. Though Isabella hadn't downed more than a glass before dinner and another during the meal, as she sat across the table from J.R. and studied him in the candlelight, she felt a definite buzz. A toasty, cozy, can't-help-smiling glow.

Ever since meeting him last spring and running into him several times since the party on New Year's at Red, she'd found herself uneasy around him. But that wasn't the case this evening.

Maybe opening up and telling him about her complicated childhood had temporarily lowered the barrier between them.

Or maybe it was the way the flecks of gold in his hazel eyes glistened in the flame that danced on the wick.

Who knew?

"I hope you saved room for lemon cake," J.R. said.

"I'm full and really ought to pass, but dinner was so good, I'd be foolish to skip dessert."

Evie had outdone herself with the grilled filet mignon, asparagus and twice-baked potatoes. No wonder J.R. had invited the talented cook to follow him to Texas. A woman with her culinary skills would be hard to replace.

"What do you have planned for tomorrow?" he asked.

"I realized that I agreed to hold off on doing anything major, but I did schedule a few of the basics, so I hope you don't mind. I have a painter coming at nine. He's bringing some color samples and will be giving me an estimate."

"That's fine," J.R. said, "as long as I can look over the colors, too."

She hadn't expected him to be quite so hands-on about the project, but it was, after all, his house. He was the boss, and he was paying her well.

"No matter how you look at it," she continued, "the fountain needs to be repaired, so the plumber will be here between ten and twelve."

"I'm okay with that. In fact, I'm looking forward to having the courtyard renovated."

Good. That was a huge relief.

"I have a plasterer coming, too. He can just give us an estimate. I didn't think that was anything you might consider major, since it's a repair that needs to be done."

"That's fine, too."

Good. If the price was right and there were no unexpected problems with the walls, the plastering could be scheduled for Monday.

Feeling a bit braver, she added, "I also asked the tile man to stop by and bring some samples. He's going to try to make it by early afternoon, but he might not arrive until closer to five. So while I'm waiting for everyone to get here, I'm going to work on one of my tapestries."

He didn't respond right away, and she tried her best not to stiffen and prepare for his objection, opting to take a positive stance instead. After all, she couldn't just vacation all week. She wanted to feel as though she'd accomplished something.

As he sat back in his seat, a slow smile stretched across his face. "You don't waste time."

"No one can accuse me of not being conscientious or practical." She returned his smile—and his question. "So how about you? What do you have planned for tomorrow?"

"I have some cutting horses being delivered in the morning. Then, sometime around noon, I'll be getting the first shipment of cattle." His eyes lit up like a child at Christmas, and she couldn't help feeling happy for him, even if she was still convinced that his attempt at ranching would be short-lived.

Evie chose that moment to bring in two slices of lemon bundt cake, a drizzle of glaze across the top. As Isabella reached for her fork, Evie filled their cups with coffee.

"Mmm," Isabella said, nearly praising the woman for the third time this evening, yet not wanting to gush. "This looks wonderful."

"Imagine what Evie could do in a fully stocked, modern kitchen," J.R. said.

Fully stocked, yes. But modern? Isabella would only go so far in compromising her vision for Molly's Pride. Of course, she wasn't going to insist that poor Evie roast beef on a spit in the fireplace or keep her perishables in a container that dangled into the well. She'd have up-to-date appliances, of course. But the focus wouldn't be on those conveniences; it would be on the two-hundred-year-old ranch house, with its white plastered walls and floors made of aged hardwood. The hacienda had a character of its own, and Isabella intended to keep it that way.

"Do you plan to work on Sunday?" J.R. asked.

"I'd like to do some weaving. Why?"

Finished with his cake, J.R. placed his napkin over his plate and leaned back in his seat. "Because I'd like to take you riding."

Her eyes widened, and she couldn't seem to keep the excitement from her voice. "You mean, on horseback?"

He chuckled. "Unless you'd rather walk or take the Jeep I just purchased."

"Oh, no. I love riding. My friend Kathy had horses and would invite me over to ride when I was in high school."

"Then why don't you plan on wrapping up your work by noon on Sunday? We'll take a picnic lunch with us."

Warning bells went off in her head. The ride he was suggesting suddenly sounded way too much like a date, and she didn't want him to get the wrong idea.

"I don't know," she said, trying to tamp down her initial enthusiasm. "I really need to get some work done."

"I think a little fresh air and some beautiful scenery will fuel your creativity."

Would it?

Maybe he hadn't meant the ride to be anything more than a tour of the ranch. And she loved horses.

She bit down lightly on her bottom lip, then studied the table. The candles flickered, and she peered at the wild roses that served as a centerpiece. The romantic ambience was wreaking havoc with her senses, as well as her resolve.

But surely this dinner wasn't a date.

This week's stay at J.R.'s ranch was strictly a business arrangement. She had a job to do, and she intended to do it as quickly and efficiently as she could. She would spend some time on the ranch, getting a feel for the place from a visitor's perspective. She would also organize the workers and outline their tasks for the times when she would be at the Fiesta and wouldn't be able to oversee them. Then it was back to her studio to finish working on the blankets and weavings she intended to sell.

Still, the thought of riding with J.R. on Sunday afternoon was tempting.

How long had it been since she'd gone riding with Kathy—or anyone else?

And he'd asked her to go on Sunday, for goodness sake. Everyone deserved a day of rest. She didn't want to do or say anything she might be sorry for later, even if she wasn't sure which answer—a yes or a no—she might regret more.

"Would it be all right if I let you know later?" she asked.

"Sure. Just give me enough time to order a picnic lunch."

She lifted the linen napkin from her lap and blotted her mouth. Then she pushed back her chair and got to her feet. As she began to pick up the plates, he stopped her. "You're a guest, Isabella. Leave those dishes here. I'll take them into the kitchen."

Their gazes met and locked. Something—pheromones, for one thing—buzzed between them with an intensity that nearly buckled her knees.

Or was it the wine she'd consumed that was doing a number on her?

Perhaps it was both.

She shrugged off the combined effect as best she could. "All right, then. If you insist…"

"I do."

She offered him a lighthearted smile. "Then, if you'll excuse me, I think I'll go to bed."

"Okay. Sleep well."

Yeah, right. Something told her that her mind was going to be swirling with a slew of possibilities in spite of all the obvious problems.

She'd set her sights on finding Mr. Right—Señor Right was more accurate—but she was afraid that J.R. Fortune thought he might be the one.

Sure, the city slicker was handsome—and wealthy. But he was also an Anglo.

A very attractive, very appealing Anglo.

But they were as different as night and day, as ill-suited as two people could be.

She'd lost herself and her family roots once, but she would never allow that to happen again.

That's why she'd made her list.

And that's why she was determined to find the right mate—and however handsome J.R. might be, he could never be that man.

So what was with her growing attraction to Mr. Wrong?

Chapter Four

The next morning passed in a blur. Isabella first met with the painter, who would have to work after the crew came in to replaster the walls. She was very specific about how she wanted him to do the wood trim and white walls. She also let him know about her plan to leave some of the old adobe showing through the plaster, giving it an authentic feel.

She'd asked the painter to use a sponge technique to make the new plaster appear aged in each of the bathrooms. He left the paint samples for her to show J.R., and she gave him a fax number to send his bid for the work.

When the plumber arrived, she took him to the courtyard and showed him the fountain. They discussed the repairs that would need to be done, and she told him to get started as soon as possible. She'd meant what she'd said about the courtyard being the focus of the home, so that was where her decorating project would begin.

The tile man had yet to arrive. She'd asked him to bring some design samples, but she'd been very specific about what she was looking for, using a couple of the projects he'd created for other people as examples.

Before heading for the loom, which she'd set up during her wait between the painter and the plumber, she went into the kitchen for a glass of water.

Baron tagged along. The rascally little pup had been underfoot all morning, but he wasn't a bother. He was both playful and cuddly—everything a happy, healthy puppy ought to be.

Isabella loved animals, especially dogs and cats. Unfortunately, her stepfather had been allergic to dander, and she hadn't been allowed to have any pets when she was a child, so having Baron around was a real treat.

In the kitchen, Evie stood at the stove, stirring something in a pot. She glanced over her shoulder at Isabella's approach.

"Something smells wonderful, Evie."

"I hope you like it. This is a tequila-lime sauce for the chicken and pasta I made."

"It sounds delicious. I'm going to gain ten pounds if I stay her much longer. Did you go to culinary school?"

Evie flushed with pleasure at the praise. "I'm afraid everything I've learned has been a result of trial and error. And believe me, there were plenty of burned pans and disappointing dishes along the way."

"Now I'm *really* impressed."

Evie beamed, then quickly glanced at the sauce simmering in the pan, running a wooden spoon along the edges. "Lunch will be ready in about twenty minutes, but I can get you a snack if you're hungry."

"I can wait. What I came for was a drink of water."

Evie reached into a cupboard, pulled out a glass and handed it to her. "There's also iced tea in the fridge, as well as soda and a variety of juices."

"Thanks, but I'll stick with water." Isabella filled her glass from the jug on the counter and took a nice, long sip. When she finished, she hung out in the kitchen, watching Evie work.

When her mom was alive, Isabella used to enjoy helping with the cooking and baking every chance she got. Of course, those days had ended way too soon, and, as a result, Isabella had never learned to cook any of her mom's dishes. Sadly, none of the recipes had been written down.

Soon after she moved to San Antonio, she'd taken a TexMex class at a cooking school that specialized in foods of the Southwest. She'd love to enroll in another one, but she'd been so busy setting up her new business that she hadn't gotten around to it.

"You know," Isabella said, "I've been meaning to thank you for putting those flowers in my room. It was a nice touch that made me feel special."

"My only job was purchasing the linens, washing them, and making up the bed. J.R. was the one who brought in the roses. He thought the room looked too sparse and bland. He said you were big on colors, and he wanted you to feel at home."

She found it interesting that he'd picked up on the fact that she liked bright colors.

"I'll have to remember to thank J.R. It was really thoughtful of him." She felt that all-too-familiar twinge of suspicion and again wondered about his motives. But, then again, he hadn't made any moves to suggest that he was interested in anything more than a client/decorator relationship.

Maybe her imagination was playing tricks on her.

"J.R. is a good man," Evie added. "One of the best. I can't believe that he's still single. He's not only handsome and wealthy, but he's goodhearted, too."

There were a lot of reasons a forty-year-old-man was still single, Isabella thought. And she wondered what J.R.'s were. Something told her he wasn't nearly as fine a person as Evie thought.

"How long have you worked for him?" Isabella asked.

"Only a couple of years, but I've known him almost twenty. My husband George and I used to own a little bistro in Malibu called the Silver Spoon. J.R. was one of our regulars. When George died, leaving me with some big medical bills, I had to sell the place. J.R. had been overseas on a business trip at the time, but when he returned and learned about my situation, he offered me a job in his kitchen. Needless to say, I took it. Then, when he decided to make the move to Texas, he asked me to join him. There's no way I would have refused."

"He must be a great employer."

"He's the best." Evie's eyes lit up. "He's also provided me with a sense of belonging, which is something I lost when my husband passed away. I really don't have a family, per se. So he's sort of become the son I never had."

"Family is important," Isabella said, repeating the truism J.R. had mentioned earlier.

And he'd been right.

Isabella's stepfather hadn't allowed her to have a relationship with the Mendozas, which was horribly unfair. She was having a difficult time forgiving him for that, no matter how good he'd been to her while she was growing up.

She supposed that was part of her stepfather's personality, though. Stan Reynolds had always been loving toward her mother, but he'd been controlling, too, and had clearly ruled the roost.

No way would Isabella let a man have that much say over her life.

"I must admit," Evie said, "I was surprised when J.R. told me he was moving to Texas. Not many men would give up a high-paying position like the one he once held and make a life-altering move the way he did."

Like Stan, her stepfather, Isabella thought. He'd get a wild notion and decide to move, whether anyone else wanted to or not.

"J.R. is certainly one of the most determined men I've ever met," Evie said.

Well, he definitely had the financial resources to make things happen.

Stan hadn't been anywhere near that wealthy, but he'd insisted on having things his way. As a result, while she was living with him, Isabella had nearly lost the essence of the person she was truly meant to be.

Evie chuckled. "I really have to hand it to him. When J.R. Fortune makes up his mind about something he wants, he goes after it. And this ranch is proof."

That it was. But Isabella still suspected he'd get tired of it all, and that this place—house, cattle and all— would be for sale within the year.

Yet she couldn't disregard the spark of excitement she'd seen in his eyes when he talked about the cattle and the horses coming.

Sometimes, she realized, when she'd caught him looking at her, she'd seen a similar spark in his eyes.

J. R. had plenty to keep him busy all day, so in spite of wanting to draw out breakfast and linger over a second cup of coffee, he'd left Isabella to do whatever needed to be done inside the house.

His first chore had been to meet the ranch foreman he'd hired last week. Well, make that both foremen.

His first interview had been with Toby Damon, a young man who'd grown up on a ranch not far from here. Toby had recently graduated from college with a degree in animal husbandry, and he'd returned to the ranch to work with his father, Frank.

Frank Damon had been a foreman on the Rocking S for years and had sacrificed to send his son to college. He'd hoped the boy would pursue a business degree and land an important white-collar job, but Toby loved the world he'd grown up in.

So his first job offer had come from his dad's employer. Things went along just fine for about six months, but then the crap hit the fan.

During Toby's interview with J.R., J.R. had taken a liking to the kid right from the start and had been impressed by his education. Yet Toby had also been upfront about the circumstances of his previous employment, which J.R. had appreciated.

But J.R. hadn't just bought the story outright. He'd made a few phone calls and was assured that Toby had been telling him the truth.

The older rancher's trophy wife had come on to Toby right after his return from school, suggesting that they engage in a discreet affair.

"It's not like she wasn't pretty," Toby had told J.R. "She was about five years older than me and had a body that would put a Hooters waitress to shame. But she was married. And she was my boss' wife. No way was I interested, and I told her so. At first, she wouldn't take no for an answer, and things got really uncomfortable. But finally, when she realized I wasn't going to buckle, she got mad. And she told her husband that I'd made a play for her."

"What did he do?"

"He fired me."

"You had a solid claim of sexual harassment. You could have sued," J.R. had told him.

"I know, but I didn't want to make trouble for my dad. He'd worked there for years, and I just couldn't risk him losing his job."

More than one of J.R.'s contacts had told him as much. From what he'd heard, Debbie Grimes wasn't just hot to look at, she was hot to trot, too.

Yesterday, J.R. had learned that Toby's dad had

resigned his position, too. Disgusted by the false allegations Debbie had made against Toby, Frank said he'd just make do until he landed another job.

Realizing that Frank was a man of principle, too, J.R. had hired him on the spot.

It was a win-win situation for all of them.

If J.R. wanted his ranch to thrive, he knew that, with his limited experience in ranching, he would need to hire men with the knowledge he lacked, men he could trust to be loyal and ethical.

After washing up in the barn, J.R. went into the house for lunch. He popped his head in the kitchen door, just to see if he could spot Isabella, but she wasn't there.

"I can serve lunch whenever you want me to," Evie told him.

"I'm ready."

"All right, but since the plumber is working on the fountain, I thought you would rather eat in the house. I set a table in the great room, if that's okay."

"It's fine. Thanks, Evie."

"Oh," the older woman said. "Isabella is in the guestroom, weaving."

"Thanks for the tip." A smile stole across J.R.'s lips. Evie, who'd worked for him long enough to know that he didn't usually take such an active role when entertaining the women he invited home—such as planning menus and picking flowers for the centerpiece—had connected the dots before Isabella had even stepped on the property.

Moments later, J.R. turned into the doorway that led to Isabella's workroom, where Baron lay on the floor, chewing on a braided and knotted piece of purple and yellow yarn. The pup glanced up at J.R., then resumed his chomping.

But it wasn't the puppy that had caught his interest. It was Isabella, with her hair sluicing down her back like a satin curtain.

He leaned against the doorjamb, watching her work.

Before long, as though she'd sensed his presence, she glanced over her shoulder. "Oh, hi. I didn't hear you."

"You seemed so intent on what you were doing, I didn't want to disturb you."

She glanced at the face of the silver bangle watch on her wrist. "I guess it's lunchtime."

"Yes, it is. Evie set a table in the great room."

He could have excused himself at that point, but he couldn't seem to tear his gaze away from the lovely Latina artisan.

As she moved about the room wearing a turquoise blouse and a pair of black jeans, he realized that her very presence added a splash of color to the house. He couldn't help thinking that, if he and Isabella were to become romantically involved, she would bring some fresh color to his world, too.

Up until a year ago, he'd been happy and perfectly content with the life he'd created for himself. He'd worked hard and played hard. And he'd enjoyed being a dyed-in-the-wool bachelor. But things had begun to change, and after he'd moved to Texas, he'd told himself that he would consider settling down if he ever found the right woman.

And now that Isabella was here, now that he'd gotten

to know her better, he suspected that she just might be that woman.

All he had to do was convince her.

That night, dinner was served in the dining room, where Evie had placed several candles to add a warm glow to the antique table that, up until two hours ago, had been gathering dust in the outbuilding. But thanks to a couple of ranch hands, it had been brought inside and polished to a high sheen.

Now, Isabella sat across from J.R., who'd poured them each a glass of red wine, as they ate another delicious meal. The food, as usual, was sumptuous, and mealtime had become something to look forward to.

The country-western background music, courtesy of a Bose stereo that had been plugged into an outlet and placed on the floor, made the atmosphere even more homey—and a little romantic.

"So," J.R. said, as he took a sip from his goblet. "How did things go this afternoon? Did the tile man ever show up?"

"Yes, finally. He left some samples for you to choose from. We can look at them after dinner."

"Good." J.R. took a roll from the linen-covered bread basket. "How about the fountain? Did the plumber run into any unexpected problems?"

"No. He expects to finish his work tomorrow. And then, assuming we choose something that's in stock, the tile man can start work on Monday morning." Isabella glanced across the table and watched J.R. spread a slab of fresh butter on his roll.

"I'm going to be pretty fussy about that fountain," he said, "so I don't want to choose something just because it's in stock."

And she *wasn't* going to be particular?

A prickle of irritation rose to the surface, and she did her best to tamp it down. "Why don't you wait and see the samples he brought. It's all high quality with old-world charm. I think you'll be able to find something you like."

"Did you see anything *you* liked?" he asked, as though her opinion might actually matter after all.

"As a matter of fact, I saw several. And one in particular."

"Then maybe we *will* be able to decide on the tile tonight." He flashed her a boyish grin that mocked her initial reaction to his male control.

Maybe he wasn't all that bossy. Maybe it was just a case of knowing how to handle him.

"Have you contacted an electrician yet?" J.R. asked.

"No, I haven't. I was under the impression that the previous owner had the house rewircd last year."

"Yes, but I'd like to have a stereo system set up so that I can pipe music into the courtyard. If you can bring someone in, I'd appreciate it." He reached for his glass of wine, and fingered the stem. "I'm not a big entertainer, but I'll definitely host a party or two on occasion, and I like music."

She glanced at the Bose stereo on the floor. Had J.R. been the one to add the background music? She'd just assumed that Evie had done so, since he'd been pretty scarce all afternoon.

Not that it mattered, she supposed, but the candlelight, as well as the music, had cast a romantic aura on their dinner.

She couldn't help thinking that J.R. intended to ask her out or make some kind of sexual overture before the night was through. And if he did, she would just have to put him in his place.

Yet the conversation didn't drift in that direction. As a result, she began to lower her guard, settling into an easy groove. Getting more comfortable.

"So," Isabella said, opting to continue the dinner conversation. "How was *your* day?"

"It was great." His eyes took on that amazing, boyish sparkle again. "The first herd of cattle arrived this morning. Now they're grazing in the south pasture. And we unloaded the cutting horses late this afternoon."

"I'd like to see them."

"They're in the barn. I'll show them to you tomorrow. Are you still up for a ride?"

Her pulse spiked a tad in anticipation, yet she glanced at the window. Outside, a branch scratched against the glass. The wind, it seemed, had kicked up this evening. Was a storm brewing?

"I'd love to go horseback riding with you," she said. "But do you think the weather will cooperate?"

"Frank, my new foreman, said it might rain a little tonight, but they're not predicting anything major. By tomorrow morning it should be clear."

"Good. And since I got a lot more weaving done today than I thought I would, my whole day is free. We can go anytime you like."

"How about eight? Is that too early?"

"No. Not at all."

He took another sip of wine, and she couldn't help looking at him, assessing him. Many women would find him attractive, with that thick head of blond hair and a roguish grin that dimpled a single cheek. No doubt, many had.

No one had to tell her he was a ladies' man. The only way a bachelor as handsome and as wealthy as J.R. Fortune had remained single until his fortieth birthday was because he wanted it that way.

Actually, his bachelorhood bothered her a bit, although she wasn't sure why.

Maybe because she had a problem with men who wouldn't commit.

Shouldn't he be happily married with a few kids by now?

Again, she suspected that his life was just the way he wanted it—unencumbered and free.

Where were all the marriage-minded men now that she'd decided to do some serious looking?

"I really like this song," he said, drawing her from her musing.

She listened carefully, catching the melody of a hit by Faith Hill, a love song called "Breathe."

"I like it, too." The very first time she'd listened to the sexy words, the heady, sensual beat, she'd decided it was the kind of song a couple could make love to.

J.R.'s gaze locked on hers, and she found herself completely caught up in awareness, in attraction.

It was the song, she told herself. The candles, the roses and the wine, too.

Yet it was even more than that. Whether she wanted to admit it or not, it was the handsome man sitting across from her, his allure so real she could almost touch it.

J.R. slid back his chair and got to his feet. A heated intensity blazed in his eyes, and for the life of her, she couldn't tear away her gaze.

He reached out his hand, as though inviting her to join him without saying a word.

She wanted to tell him no, to set him straight about their business relationship. Yet, for some wild and crazy reason, she took the hand he'd offered and let him slowly draw her to her feet.

Mesmerized—by the song, by the words, by the heat in his gaze—she found herself slipping into his arms and swaying to the music. Their bodies melded, their hearts beat in time. As their scents mingled, a slow and steady rush whizzed through Isabella, rivaling the one Faith sang about.

When the song ended, J.R. continued to hold her, to move slowly to a silent beat.

She wasn't sure where this was going, wasn't sure what she would do about it. And while she should have pushed away, ending it before it got completely out of hand, she couldn't bring herself to do it. Not yet. It felt too good. So she held on tight until he finally—and, maybe, reluctantly?—released her.

Unable to help herself, she tilted her face, her gaze seeking his.

Passion simmered in his eyes.

Oh, wow. He was about to kiss her, which should have scared the daylights out of her, since it would definitely complicate any plans she had for her future, as well as the business arrangement they'd entered.

Yet instead of uttering any kind of objection, her heart pounded to beat the band, and her hormones blared out of control.

Yes, he was definitely going to kiss her; she was sure of it.

But he didn't.

In a surprise move, he reached out and touched her hair, letting a silky strand sluice through his fingers.

"Thanks for the dance," he said.

Her heart was now pounding so hard she could hear it thunder in her ears.

She wouldn't have allowed him to kiss her, although she'd been sorely tempted.

Liar, a small voice whispered.

If she'd truly planned to push him away, then why was she standing here like a love-struck adolescent, drowning in a sea of disappointment?

Chapter Five

J.R. woke early on Sunday morning and made his way to the kitchen, where Evie had brewed a fresh pot of coffee and baked a batch of cranberry-orange muffins.

It had taken everything he had not to kiss Isabella senseless last night, but he knew she had reservations about getting involved with him, although he wasn't exactly sure why. She clearly wanted him as badly as he wanted her—there were some things a man just knew.

So he'd drawn out the dance and the near-kiss, a decision that had nearly backfired on him, since he hadn't realized how hard it would be for him to refrain.

In truth, it had just about killed him to settle for anything less than a sweet, gentle assault of her lips and mouth, but that had been a part of his plan. He'd wanted to set off a longing in Isabella that would make her want to progress to a physical level so badly that she'd stop fighting herself.

Trouble was, it had set off a longing in him that had kept him up for hours last night and had awoken him before dawn, eager to start the day.

"Good morning," Evie said, handing him a steaming mug of fresh-brewed coffee. "How did things go last night?"

He smiled. "As well as I'd hoped." It's not as though he'd discussed details with Evie either before or after dinner, but he'd inadvertently clued her in prior to Isabella's arrival by telling her that he wanted to make his new decorator feel welcome.

Evie had worked for him long enough to be able to fill in the blanks, especially when J.R. started picking roses for the guestroom and lighting candles.

And no. He hadn't gone to that much trouble to impress a woman in California—nor had he needed to—but Isabella was different from anyone he'd ever dated in the past.

"Is the picnic lunch ready to go?" he asked.

"Yes, it's all packed. I even found an old basket in one of the cupboards that you can carry it in. If you're anything like my husband, George, you'll probably scoff at carrying your lunch in anything other than a brown paper bag, but the basket is sweet. And it will definitely please Isabella." Evie smiled. "I had a little fun decorating it, too. No one appreciates romance more than I do."

J.R. tossed her grin right back at her, trusting that she'd done him proud. He'd no more than taken another sip of coffee when Isabella stepped into the kitchen, wearing a breezy smile that made her eyes dance.

A pair of stylish jeans molded over her hips, and a tailored yellow blouse she'd tucked in showed off a small waist. Her hair had been swept into a twist on the back of her head and was held in place with a bulky silver clip.

Too bad, he thought. He'd been having some Lady Godiva fantasies last night when he thought of Isabella on horseback, and her long, flowing hair had been a big part of them.

A renewed smile, triggered by Isabella's entrance and the renewal of his fantasy, spread across J.R.'s face.

"You were right about the rain," Isabella said. "It only sprinkled a bit last night. The ground is damp, but the sky is clear and sunny."

"It's going to be a nice day for a ride." He took a mug from the cupboard and poured her some coffee.

"Thank you." She took the cup with both hands and lifted it to her nose. Then she closed her eyes, as though savoring the aroma of the fresh morning brew.

There were plenty of things he could be doing right now, but none of them were as intriguing as standing here, watching her.

"You know," she said. "I'd meant to show you the paint and tile samples last night."

She didn't have to say why she hadn't. The kiss they'd nearly shared had left them both unbalanced.

As their gazes met, her cheeks flushed, convincing him he'd been right. But with Evie in the room, he decided to let the memory drop, at least for the moment.

"We can look the samples over after our ride," he said.

"Good idea." Isabella reached for the creamer and poured a bit into her cup. Then she added a spoonful of sugar.

He nodded toward the counter, where a plate of warm muffins awaited. "Why don't you have a bit to eat while I see to the horses."

"All right, but I won't be long. If you want to wait for me, I'll eat quickly."

J.R. leaned against the kitchen counter. "Take your time."

Five minutes later, with the picnic basket Evie had packed in one hand, J.R. walked Isabella out to the barn.

Just outside the newly repaired door, Frank and Toby stood, each drinking coffee—no doubt from the pot they kept in their quarters.

"Hey, boss." Frank smiled and tipped his hat to Isabella. "Good mornin', ma'am."

J.R. placed his hand on the small of Isabella's back as he introduced her to his key employees. He supposed the possessive touch was his way of letting the men know he'd laid his claim on her—at least, in a way.

Or maybe he just wanted to touch her again, now that they'd shared a sensual dance and had held each other close.

Isabella offered the men a pretty smile. "It's nice to meet you."

"Toby and I saddled those horses for you. That buckskin mare was a good choice. And so was the chestnut gelding."

"Thanks, Frank."

"You're welcome. Toby and I are heading into Red Rock this morning. A couple of the cowboys from our old spread are going to meet with us for breakfast. They're good men, and I heard they might be looking for work."

"We can certainly use a few more hands. Have them come talk to me tomorrow morning."

Frank nodded. "I'll do that, boss. Thanks."

As the men headed toward the ranch pickup, J.R. again placed his hand on Isabella's back and guided her toward the barn. "Come on. Let's go."

They found the horses saddled and waiting. After leading them through the newly repaired door, J.R. sensed that Isabella might have trouble mounting.

"Need a boost?" he asked.

"Yes. Do you mind?"

"Not at all." J.R. clasped his hands together, making a step for her foot.

She took the reins in one hand and gripped the saddle horn with the other. As she mounted, he relished the scent of her, something distinctly feminine that hinted of exotic flowers.

Once she was atop the mare, he climbed into the saddle, and they both took off. As they approached the nearest corral, where they'd turned out the cutting horses yesterday, he pointed them out.

"They're beautiful," Isabella said.

J.R. wouldn't go that far. But the horses were sure-footed and well-trained. Purchasing them had made him feel as though he really was a rancher, as though his dream was finally coming together.

"Let's head this way." J.R. urged the gelding to the right, and Isabella followed.

They rode to the pasture, where the first cattle now grazed. He had another load coming on Tuesday, so the men Frank had told him about would come in handy, if he ended up hiring them.

"Are you glad you made such a big change in your life?" Isabella asked.

"Absolutely." As he studied the herd in the field, his heart swelled with pride. "Now, that's what I call beautiful."

"Beef cows?" she asked. "Not the horses?"

"Yep." He slid her a glance. "Do you think I'm crazy?"

She laughed. "At times? Yes, it's crossed my mind. You had it all in Los Angeles."

"No," he said. "I came close to having it all in L.A. But this is the real thing."

And, when it came to women, to partners who could weather the storms of life, as his parents had, he had a feeling Isabella was the real thing, too.

After checking on the cattle, they rode along the property line of his ranch, and he pointed out where his ranch ended and his closest neighbor's began.

Birds chirped in the treetops, and a pleasant breeze rustled the leaves. By the time they'd ridden along the creek to the lake, it was growing close to eleven.

"Why don't we stop here and have lunch," he said.

"Sounds good to me."

The sun had dried most of the dampness from the ground, yet J.R. searched for a perfect spot, settling on a grassy knoll. When he opened the basket Evie had packed, he found a red vinyl tablecloth, which he spread on the ground in lieu of a blanket. "Let's sit on this. That way we won't get muddy."

Before long, the horses were grazing in the new green grass, and J.R. had a feast set before them: fried chicken, potato salad, fresh strawberries and chocolate cupcakes.

"Evie's worth her weight in gold," Isabella said. "I hope you're paying her well."

"I am, but she's more than an employee." Evie had become nearly as supportive as his mother had been—and just as easy to talk to. She'd lost her husband about the same time J.R.'s mom had died, so they'd shared their grief and helped each other work through it.

J.R. and Isabella ate in silence for a while. Then he asked, "Who did you hire to look after your studio?"

"Her name is Sarah. She's the daughter of one of my dad's neighbors. She comes by the studio and hangs out sometimes. She's young and just out of high school, but she has a real interest in art. So I've been encouraging her to take some classes at the local junior college."

"It sounds like a perfect setup."

"Well…" Isabella lifted one of the red napkins, dabbed it at her mouth then wiped her hands. "I'm kind of like a worried mama with my business. I find myself calling to check up on her all the time."

"I'm sure she'll do fine."

"Either way, I'm going to have to spend a lot of time burning up the highway. It's tough to be in two places at once, but I really need to be a presence at the Fiesta. Hopefully, by the time it starts next week, I'll have everything lined up here and won't need to spend every minute at the ranch."

"I understand. And while I'm in a hurry to get things done, feel free to put some things off until you *can* spend every minute here."

She shot him a *what*-did-you-say? glance.

He shrugged a single shoulder and slipped her a crooked grin. "You're different than any woman I've ever met."

"How so?"

He'd like to tell himself that Isabella was just another pretty face, just another potential relationship, but he didn't buy that.

The more time he spent with her, the more drawn to her he felt. This could be the real thing.

"You have an exotic beauty that captivates me. And I'm in awe of your artistic ability. I'm intrigued by you, and I'd like to get to know you better."

She seemed a bit stymied by what he'd admitted. And maybe he'd confessed too soon. But he wasn't the only one dealing with interest and attraction, and the sooner they both admitted it, the better.

When they finished eating and it was time to head back to the ranch, J.R. packed the remnants of their lunch into the basket. Then they walked to the horses that were grazing in the sweet grass nearby.

The mare lifted her head as Isabella approached and snorted, as if saying, "Aw, do we have to?"

J.R. felt the same way. They'd shared an idyllic morning, and he hated to see it end.

She reached for the reins, as well as the saddle

horn, then glanced over her shoulder. "Can you give me a boost?"

"Sure." He threaded his fingers together to provide a step for her, but as she placed her foot into his hands, her other leg seemed to give way and she stumbled, falling against him.

Thrown off balance by the unexpected shift in weight, J.R. lost his footing, and the two of them tumbled onto the rain-softened ground.

He rolled to his side, bracing himself on his elbow, and raised up to look her over, hoping she hadn't gotten hurt. When her eyes met his, a belly laugh erupted from deep inside her, and he couldn't help laughing himself.

"I stepped in a gopher hole," she said. "Did I hurt you?"

"Just my pride. I was trying to be gallant."

Her hair had come out of the clip. At least, part of it had. The other half was tangled in it. He brushed a loose strand away from her brow.

Her laughter ceased, and a serious expression stole over her face, chasing away any sign of playfulness. Something simmered in her eyes. That same something that told him she'd been expecting him to kiss her last night, that she'd actually wanted him to.

But right this moment, any careful planning he'd done in the past no longer mattered. Not when he had an overwhelming urge to kiss her.

As he should have done last night.

Isabella hadn't expected to fall into J.R.'s arms, to roll onto her back and find him hovering over her with desire brewing in his eyes.

That kiss they'd nearly shared last night was going to take place today, even if she had to make the first move.

Perhaps her senses had been jarred silly. But right now, neither her list nor her good sense seemed to matter.

Just one kiss, she told herself. What would it hurt? A kiss was a great way to judge whether a couple had any chemistry at all.

Perhaps it would be disappointing. After all, there had to be a reason a man as handsome and as wealthy as J.R. Fortune was still single at the age of forty.

Being a lousy lover was certainly a possibility.

But as he brushed his lips across hers, as he nipped playfully at her mouth, baiting her, urging her on, her lips parted, and all bets were off.

The kiss deepened, and something raw, something dangerously compelling took over, as need exploded into a heady rush.

He slid his tongue inside her mouth, exploring, seeking, tasting.

Unable and unwilling to put a stop to the sweet assault, she kissed him back with all she had, combing her fingers through his hair, gripping him with a quiet desperation.

Never had she felt such need, such desire.

Why? she asked. Why with a man who wasn't her type? And J.R. Fortune was *so* not her type.

Was she crazy? She pushed against his chest, and his heartbeat pulsed against her fingers.

So much for him being a lousy lover. If that one little kiss had the power to turn her senses inside out and make her consider having sex in a field of wildflowers, what effect would foreplay have on her? Or the act itself?

Oh, for Pete's sake. What in the world was she thinking? Her uncontrollable reaction was enough to scare the dickens out of her.

In their carefree youth, her young parents had shared a passionate, ill-fated relationship, and look where following their hormones had gotten them—married to the wrong person.

Divorced with a two-year-old child.

And speaking of children, J.R. wasn't the man with whom she wanted to create a family, the man with whom she wanted to grow old.

"I'm sorry," she said. "I can't. This wasn't…"

"Don't tell me it wasn't good for you." His smile told her that he would know the truth from a lie.

Still, she couldn't help but deny the effects. Or, at least, put them in perspective.

"Okay, as far as kisses go, it was pretty good. But it wasn't what you thought it was." She rolled to the side, scrambled to her knees and stood.

"What did I think it was?" He remained sprawled out on the grass, braced up on his elbow. He continued to grin, as though he knew something she didn't.

She reached for the silver clip that was now tangled in her hair. "Well, I'm not exactly sure what you thought. But, for the record, I'm not interested in having a romantic relationship."

He still didn't appear to be in any hurry to rise. "Actually, we hit that kiss out of the ballpark. And since you were an active participant, I'm surprised that you want to fight the feeling."

Why had she let her hormones rule her head?

She tore her gaze away from him and tried to open the hair clip and tug it free from the tangled strands, but the more she worked at it, the more stuck and knotted it became.

Ironically, that's the kind of situation in which she'd just found herself: the harder she tried to get free, the more convoluted the whole mess seemed.

"Okay," she finally said. "You're a great kisser. And since it's been a long time since I've kissed anyone, it was easy to lose my head. But that doesn't mean I want to get involved with you."

"Why not?"

She couldn't tell him the real reason without risking her job or hurting his feelings.

How would he respond if she told him her actual reservations—that she didn't want to get involved with him because he was a city slicker? That he not only belonged in California, but that he would surely return there when his whim to be a rancher faded?

Giving the clip another tug and feeling a sting of pain at her scalp, she took a deep breath and gave him another answer, one that was both logical and reasonable. "I don't mix business with pleasure. And since you're my client, I'd like to keep our arrangement strictly business."

When she gave the clip another unsuccessful tug, she groaned, and J.R. got to his feet.

He strode toward her, that amused grin still splashed across his face. "Let me help."

She didn't want his help. She didn't want anything except to go back to the ranch and pretend that this had never happened.

Without much effort, J.R. managed to take the clip out of her hair and hand it to her with a bemused smile. "You look especially pretty when you're flustered."

She didn't feel one bit pretty. Her hair, which was half up and half down, was now a tangled mess. And her clothes were damp and dirty, especially her knees, hips and back, all of which had touched the rain-soaked ground.

"I'm not really flustered," she said, willing the words to be true. "It's just the adrenaline that kicked in during the fall. I'll be fine as soon as I climb on my horse."

But something told her she wouldn't be fine for a long, long time.

The adrenaline—or whatever the heck it really was—hadn't kicked in until J.R. had hovered over her with a heated expression that stole her breath away, until they'd kissed and her world had spun out of control.

A world that was still spinning like crazy.

J.R. and Isabella tiptoed around that kiss for the rest of the day and evening. Then, after a quiet dinner, she reminded him that they hadn't yet looked over the paint and tile samples that had been left at the house.

After the table had been cleared, she laid them out for him to see.

J.R. furrowed his brow and lifted one of the paint samples. "They're all white. What kind of color choice is this?"

"Actually, the one you have in your hand is called Eggshell." She pointed to another. "And this one is Sweet Cream."

He returned the card to the table. "Don't you think we need some color on the walls?"

Not if they were going to maintain an authentic feel to the house. She placed her hands on her hips, annoyed that he was questioning her sense of style. "I'm going to add color by way of the fabrics, wall coverings and decorator items."

No way would she agree to paint those beautiful, old plaster walls any color but white.

They appeared to be at an impasse until he shrugged. "It's not as though I wanted you to choose something red or purple for the walls. It's just that these will be boring."

"I'll use plenty of color in the house," she said. "Didn't you read my proposal?"

"Yes, but I thought some of those items would be left to negotiation, after your week here is up."

"What's wrong with white walls and splashes of color throughout?"

He seemed to ponder that for a while, then shrugged. "Okay, you're the expert."

She hadn't expected him to put up a fight about having plain plaster walls, but at least he'd yielded, which was a good sign.

"So we can go with white walls?" she asked.

He scrunched his face. "All right. But I can't tell a difference between these samples. Not really. You go ahead and pick whichever one you want."

She hated to feel smug about winning something so simple, so she stifled a grin and laid out the tiles that Ernesto Ramos had left with her yesterday.

Of all the samples Ernesto had brought, Isabella had

chosen four. She placed her favorite down first, followed by the others in order of her preference.

J.R. pointed to the last one. "This is nice."

"I think so, too," she said, although that particular tile design had been her last choice. She placed her index finger on her bottom lip, as though really giving it a lot of thought. Then she pointed to her favorite, which had a white background with a blue and yellow design. "How about this one? It has a lot of old-world charm."

"I don't know..."

"What's wrong with it?" she asked.

"There's nothing *wrong* with it. It's just that I like the other one better. I can see red flowers in the courtyard, and this one has red in the design."

He had a point, she supposed. It was, after all, his house, his fountain. And ultimately his choice. But there was something about this particular project that made her want to take a more active role in the décor.

Or was it that she just didn't want to yield to J. R. Fortune?

Unwilling to ponder that thought, she reminded herself again that it was his house, and that he was the client. "All right. Can I tell Ernesto that we'd like this one?"

J.R. nodded, and the choice had been made.

Yet that still didn't help her sleep any better that night than the one before.

Bright and early on Monday morning, Isabella drove back to San Antonio to check on Sarah Weatherford, the eighteen-year-old woman who was looking after her studio.

Sarah, a petite redhead with green eyes and a scatter

of freckles across her nose, lived in the house across the street from Isabella's father. The young woman had been going through a difficult time, thanks to a boyfriend who'd dumped her for a college coed he'd met on campus.

The breakup alone would have been tough for anyone to deal with, but Sarah, who'd struggled with learning disabilities for years, had taken it especially hard because she'd always considered college to be out of her reach.

Yet in spite of just limping through high school, she'd excelled in art classes. When she heard that an artisan had opened a studio in the neighborhood, she'd come by to visit and to introduce herself to Isabella.

Sarah had been impressed with the weavings and in awe of Isabella's talent. In time, Isabella had been able to talk Sarah into enrolling in an art course at the junior college.

The class had done wonders for Sarah's self-esteem, and so had Isabella's request for Sarah to watch over the studio in her absence.

After arriving at her father's house in San Antonio, Isabella met with Sarah and discussed her plans for the upcoming week—preparing for Fiesta. Then she checked messages and returned phone calls. She saved the best for last, calling her friend, Jane Gilliam, who would soon marry Isabella's cousin, Jorge Mendoza.

She dialed the Red Rock Readingworks, then waited for Jane to get on the line.

"Can you sneak away for lunch?" Jane asked.

"I'd love to."

"Great. I have a meeting this morning, but it should be over by noon. I'll see you at Red."

Isabella always enjoyed her time with Jane, but she especially looked forward to talking to her today. She needed someone to confide in, someone she could trust to listen, to understand and to offer advice. This "thing" with J.R. had gotten way too complicated, and she could use her friend's perspective.

As was her habit, Isabella arrived at the restaurant early, hoping to snag a table in the courtyard. Unfortunately, they were all occupied, and she had to take one in the main dining room.

She'd no more than settled into her chair when the busboy served two glasses of water, chips and salsa.

Jane arrived moments later and took the seat across from her. The women chatted a few minutes about the meeting Jane had just left.

"So how are things going with the new decorating project?" Jane asked.

"Actually?" Isabella tried to smile, but it fell flat. "It's…a bit troubling."

"Why?"

Isabella snagged a chip and popped it into her mouth, the crunch doing little to ease the tension she'd been feeling ever since J.R. had kissed her. "I think J.R. is interested in more than decorating his home."

Jane leaned forward, her eyes sparking. "Really? Lucky you."

Isabella shook her head. "No, I'm *not* lucky. J.R. is the last guy I'd date. He's not my type."

"You mean there isn't any chemistry?"

She sighed. "I wish there weren't, but I let him kiss me yesterday, hoping to prove a point to myself. And, *unfortunately,* our chemistry level is off the charts."

"What's wrong with that?" Jane leaned back in her seat with a grin that looked suspiciously smug. "Chemistry is definitely important and should be high on your list."

Isabella had left it off the list completely. "I thought if a man had all the other qualities, the chemistry would be a given."

"That's not always the case."

"Okay, so I was a little naive. But J.R. still isn't my type."

Jane reached for a chip and dipped it into the salsa. But instead of eating it, she held it upright like the pointer a professor used during a lecture. "If I recall some of those things on your list, J.R. definitely ought to be in the running."

"I wanted a man with a steady job and his feet planted firmly on the ground. Leaving L.A. and launching a new career at J.R.'s age reeks of midlife crisis."

Jane leaned forward, that chip still raised. "The guy is wealthy, Isabella. I'd consider that stable and dependable. What more could you want?"

"Okay, he might dress like a successful Texas rancher, but he's used to traveling in much more sophisticated circles. And I'm not."

"You're no slouch in a social setting. And with your business taking off the way it is, you'd better get used to moving in those dreaded circles."

Isabella fingered her napkin, rolling the corner, as she pondered the truth of Jane's statement. Then she glanced across the table. "You're my best friend. You're supposed to let me vent and tell me that I'm right."

A knowing smile spread across Jane's face. "Even if I think you're wrong?"

"Ever since you fell head over heels for Jorge, you've had stars in your eyes. But love has nothing to do with this. I'm just terribly attracted to J.R. for some reason. And to make matters worse, he's forty and has never been married. That clearly means he's a perpetual bachelor at heart and afraid to commit."

"No, it doesn't. Look at Jorge. Now there was a perpetual bachelor. But he fell in love with me, and let me tell you, the man is definitely committed, and I couldn't be happier."

Isabella slumped in her seat, something her stepdad used to pester her about. Something she rarely did anymore.

"Do you know what I think?" Jane asked.

"What?"

"I think you're the one who's afraid to commit."

Isabella had to chew on that for a while.

"Maybe you should burn that perfect-mate list," Jane added.

The waiter chose that moment to take their orders.

"I'll have the TexMex salad," Isabella said.

Jane chose a chicken tostada.

After the waiter left, Isabella relented. "Okay, I admit that I'm probably being foolish. But there's still something holding me back."

"What's that?"

"I'm not attracted to Anglos, remember?"

"Apparently, you're attracted to *this* one."

Isabella blew out a sigh. Jane wasn't helping at all. "Okay. So it's really not the Anglo thing. It's just that my heritage is an important part of me, and I want someone who can appreciate my Tejana roots, someone who will share my traditions. I'm not sure a man who isn't Latino will do that."

"It depends on the man," Jane said. "I'll bet J.R. can. After all, he's letting you decorate his house, so he's definitely going with your style."

"I don't know about that. He hasn't given me a lot of freedom, and we don't always see eye to eye. If truth be told, I suspect that he awarded me this job to keep me close to him. Why else would he insist that I spend the week there?"

"Maybe he's falling for you and wants an opportunity to see what develops. If so, I think you should feel flattered."

Actually, if that had been J.R.'s motivation, it was a bit too much like her stepfather's attempt to keep her mom all to himself, to cut her off from the Mendozas.

Isabella placed her elbows on the table, leaned forward and spoke quietly. "I think he's enamored with an image of me, although I have no clue what image that is."

Jane smiled. "Every woman deserves to be held in high esteem by the man she loves."

"But that's just it," Isabella said. "I *don't* love him."

"Why don't you give him a chance to change your mind?"

Isabella couldn't do that. What if he were able to sweep her off her feet? Then what?

Or what if she did let things progress and he decided to sell the ranch and head back to Los Angeles? No way would she consider either a move or a long-distance relationship. Not when she'd finally found herself—in Texas.

"Maybe you should just let things ride and see what happens," Jane said.

But Isabella wasn't so sure. What if she lost herself all over again?

Chapter Six

On Wednesday, as the sun began to sink low in the sky, J.R. used his arm to wipe the sweat off his brow. He'd been working with Toby and Frank since just after noon on a stretch of fence in the south pasture. He had a second shipment of cattle coming tomorrow morning, and this is where they would graze.

Baron crouched in the grass, his tail wagging as he sniffed and growled at something—a bug, no doubt. At five months old, he was really too small to be of any help, but J.R. had grown attached to the little guy and liked having him around. Besides, he was going to be a ranch dog, so he might as well get used to riding with the hands.

Had Isabella not taken off for San Antonio on Monday, J.R. might have left Baron in the house with her. She'd really taken to the pup, which seemed like a good sign.

Too bad she didn't claim the same affection for J.R.

Actually, he suspected that she was feeling a hell of a lot more than she admitted. He'd seen it in her eyes—both before and after that kiss.

In all of his adult years and even before that, he'd rarely been attracted to a woman who didn't find him appealing and didn't at least consider having a relationship of one kind or another. On the contrary, it was usually J.R. who put the brakes on.

So why was Isabella holding back?

A lesser man might have let her go, telling himself there were other fish in the sea, but when J.R. set his sights on something, he didn't let anything stand in his way.

And now that he'd kissed Isabella, now that he'd experienced her passionate response, he was even more determined than ever to pursue her.

He wasn't entirely sure what he was feeling for her, but it was definitely more than just a little attraction. Not that he'd call it love, but he'd never been involved with a woman who turned him every which way but loose. Isabella, though, was coming pretty damn close.

"Well," Frank said, lifting his hat long enough to wipe his forehead with a red handkerchief, "looks like we got 'er done. This ought to hold 'em."

J.R. studied the repaired fencing and nodded his approval. There was nothing like a good workout that produced not only results, but plenty of sweat.

"I'll load up the pickup," Frank said. "And then we can head back to the ranch."

Toby, who'd been overseeing work on the well and had joined Frank and J.R. after they'd gotten started on the fence, had ridden one of the horses out to the pasture. "Baron and I'll meet you there."

"Do you think he can keep up with you?" J.R. asked. "He's still pretty young."

"It's not that far. If he tuckers out, I'll pick him up and let him ride with me."

Everyone, it seemed, had grown fond of that rascally pup, and Toby was no exception.

Baron growled again, then bravely barked and snapped at the grasshopper he'd found. He'd been napping for the past hour, so he was probably raring to go.

"Go ahead," J.R. said.

Toby helped load the tools and extra fencing material into the bed of the truck, which was parked along the county road, next to where they'd been working. Then he mounted his horse and called Baron.

The pup wagged his tail and followed Toby's gelding through the field and toward the barn.

J.R. and Frank slipped between the barbed-wire strands and climbed into J.R.'s pickup. They'd just reached the house when Isabella pulled up.

"I'll take care of putting away these tools," Frank said.

"Thanks. I appreciate that." J.R. watched as Isabella slid out of the driver's seat, wearing a lime-green blouse and a pair of white slacks. Her hair hung down her back, long and silky, just the way he liked it.

When she'd left on Monday morning, she'd said she would be back, and he'd known she would. Still, things had been pretty awkward between them after the kiss, so seeing her again was a pleasant surprise.

"How were things at the studio?" he asked.

"It's been pretty quiet. Sarah assured me that she has everything under control."

"That's got to be comforting." J.R. knew that if he were to leave the ranch, Frank and Toby could handle anything that came their way. And that if there were any questions, they'd call and run things by him for approval.

Isabella swept a strand of hair behind her shoulder. "It's a bit of a relief, I suppose. But I tend to be a control freak, and it's hard for me to let go, although I guess I'll have to get used to that. If my business continues to grow, I'll have to rely on others to help out."

If she began hanging out at the ranch more, she'd also need to leave Sarah in charge more often.

Isabella nodded toward the house. "How did the plastering go today?"

"I have no idea." J.R. held up his dirty hands. "I've been working on the south fence all afternoon."

She reached for her purse and shut the driver's-side door. "I'm going to check and make sure the workers did what I asked them to do."

"I'll come in with you," he said. "I'd like to see what they've done, too."

He'd also decided that he would have to keep an eye on Isabella. He liked her overall plans for the house and had refused to consider another decorator, but he didn't want to give her too much freedom.

A few antiques were fine—and so were some of the leftover paintings and artwork. But Isabella seemed intent on maintaining the original hacienda aura, and while he could appreciate her vision, he didn't want to end up residing in a living history museum, which just might happen if he left her on her own.

"Where's Baron?" she asked. "I've missed that little guy."

J.R. tossed her a smile. "Baron's with Toby. He's been learning how to be a ranch dog. Before you know it, he'll be herding cattle for us."

"That's hard to imagine," Isabella said, as the two of them started for the house.

They didn't get more than a few steps, when they heard Toby shouting, "Boss!"

There was a tinge of panic in his voice, as he rode up to J.R., holding the puppy in his arms.

"Baron got hurt," Toby said. *"Bad."*

J.R.'s heart dropped to his gut. Damn. He should have insisted that the pup ride back in the truck. "What happened?"

"When I stopped at the gate, he nipped at the gelding's hoof. Ol' Smokey wasn't in the mood for games and kicked him in the head. Baron was knocked out. He came to, but he's loopy."

J.R. reached for the limp puppy. A wave of fear and concern swept over him. The wound had turned the white fur on his head bloodred.

Baron whimpered as he was transferred from Toby's arms to J.R.'s.

"I hope we don't need to put him down," Toby said.

J.R. felt the same way. He knew that putting an animal out of its misery was a real—and sad—part of ranch life, but he sure hoped it wouldn't be necessary with Baron. And it wasn't just because the pup had good bloodlines. J.R. had grown attached to the little guy—apparently even more than he realized.

"I'll take him to the vet," J.R. said. "It's not quite five, so will you give Dr. Eldridge a call and tell him we're on our way?"

Toby climbed off his horse. "I'll do it right now. You know where the office is, right?"

"Yes, I do. Ethan, the doctor, is an old friend of mine."

A couple of weeks before, J.R. had stopped by Ethan's office and told him he'd moved to Red Rock and would be using his services someday. He just hadn't expected the doctor's first patient to be Baron.

"If he's a mobile vet," Isabella said, "maybe we should call him out here."

"It'll be faster if we take Baron to him." J.R. just hoped Ethan wasn't away from the office and on a call. But if he was, he'd have a veterinary technician on duty who might be able to help.

As J.R. started for his truck, Isabella placed her hand on his forearm, momentarily stopping him. Her whiskey-brown eyes were filled with compassion. "I'm going with you. Do you want me to hold him? Or should I drive?"

Surprised that she'd offered, yet appreciative, J.R. thanked her then added, "If you don't mind holding him, I'll ask Evie to bring out a towel."

"There's no time for that." Isabella reached for the dog, gently taking him into her arms. "Since you know where you're going, you drive."

J.R. nodded, then rushed toward the truck. After they climbed into the cab, he started the engine and put the transmission into gear. He glanced in his rearview mirror long enough to back up the vehicle and turn around. Then they were off.

Once they were on the county road and headed toward Red Rock, he stole a look at Isabella, who held the pup in her arms. Blood from Baron's head had stained her blouse, yet she didn't seem to mind.

Had Molly Fortune been alive and at the ranch just minutes ago, she wouldn't have given her clothing a second thought, either. She would have put a hurt child or an injured animal first.

He was suddenly struck by their similarities. Of course, when it came to appearance, Isabella didn't resemble Molly in the least. But the fact that they shared some of the same admirable character qualities was hard to ignore.

J.R. still wasn't sure exactly what he was feeling for Isabella. But at that very moment, he realized that whatever it was had grown beyond mere sexual attraction.

Isabella glanced down at the puppy she held in her arms, his body as flaccid as a wrung-out dishrag. Yet he raised his head slightly, and his eyes opened. He whimpered before settling back into her arms. It broke her heart to see him hurt and in pain.

"How's he doing?" J.R. asked, as he focused on the road ahead.

"I'm not sure. The bleeding stopped, so that's good." She placed two fingers on Baron's chest, feeling for a pulse. It seemed to be steady, but what did she know? She had very little knowledge of first aid of any kind—human or canine.

"Thanks for coming with me," J.R. said, his gaze snagging hers and making her feel like some kind of teammate.

Strangely, right at this moment, she'd fallen easily into that role. "I knew you'd need someone to hold him while you drove."

J.R. glanced at her chest, where a splotch of red had smeared with brown. "I'm afraid you might never get that bloodstain out."

She'd thought about that, but only after she'd taken the puppy in her arms. Yet that didn't seem to matter in the scheme of things. Clothing was replaceable, and while some people might believe that animals were, too, Isabella wasn't one of them. So she shrugged and offered him a wistful grin. "I'll try soaking it when I get home."

J.R. returned his attention to the road, and ten minutes later, they arrived at the veterinarian's office.

Dr. Ethan Eldridge, a tall, tanned man in his late thirties or early forties, had been expecting them, thanks to Toby's phone call, and met them in the waiting room. "I was just about to lock up and head home, so I'm glad you caught me."

The vet led them to an exam room, and Isabella carefully laid the puppy on the small, stainless-steel examining table. Baron lifted his head slightly and looked at Isabella, his eyes glassy.

She couldn't help remembering how spunky he'd been, how he would growl as he chewed on the knotted yarn she'd made him. How he'd tag after her from room to room. How he'd lick her face whenever she picked him up. Seeing him this way brought tears to her eyes.

As the doctor examined the puppy they'd both grown to care about, Isabella and J.R. stood back, watching.

The vet tech, a young woman in her early twenties, came in. Moments later, she and the doctor took Baron back for an X ray.

"Now I know how my parents felt the night I got hurt during a high school football game," J.R. said.

Isabella turned to him, saw him standing with his brow furrowed, his arms crossed. She tried to imagine him as a teenager, a football player. She assumed he'd been popular, especially with the girls.

"What happened?" she asked, wanting to know what he'd been like when he was younger.

"I was a running back, going out for a swing pass, and took a hard hit from both the safety and a defensive end. I was knocked unconscious, and they had to carry me off the field."

"Head injuries are scary," Isabella said.

"That's what my mom always used to say. She was a real trooper whenever my brothers or I needed stitches or a cast. But a little concussion sure shook her up."

Isabella could see why it would and flashed him a knowing smile. "It sounds to me as though she was a typical mom."

"In some ways, I guess she was, but she was also unique. Special." His mind seemed to drift into memory mode, as he glanced down at the floor. Then his gaze lifted, meeting hers. "You remind me of her."

"I do? In what way?"

He shrugged, as though he hadn't really given it a

whole lot of thought. Or maybe because he didn't want to discuss their similarities.

The door swung open, and Dr. Eldridge returned alone. Isabella braced herself, afraid they were about to hear a grim prognosis.

"The good news is that there isn't a skull fracture," Dr. Eldridge said.

"And the bad news?" J.R. asked.

"Baron has a serious concussion, and I'd like to keep him overnight for observation."

"But he'll be okay?" J.R.'s brow furrowed again, his worry and concern for the puppy obvious.

As Isabella took note of this tender side of J.R. and how much he cared for the little dog, it touched her in a way she hadn't expected.

"I don't foresee any reason why he won't be back to his playful self in the next couple of days," Dr. Eldridge said. "We'll keep him quiet and sedated this evening. If all goes well, he can go home tomorrow."

J.R. thanked the doctor, taking time to introduce him to Isabella. Then J.R. asked about the vet's wife, Susan.

Isabella quickly put two and two together, realizing that she'd met Susan on several occasions. Susan Fortune Eldridge was J.R.'s cousin; their fathers had been brothers.

Susan, who had a PhD in psychology, once worked for a national hotline that specialized in troubled teens. Now she was employed by the Fortune Foundation, doing the same kind of outreach at a local level.

"Susan's doing great," Ethan said. "You'll have to come out to the ranch and visit one day soon."

"I'd like that." J.R. turned to Isabella. "Ethan owns a gentleman's ranch."

"I'm afraid I was raised in the city," she said. "So I'm not exactly sure what that is."

"It's smaller than a working ranch, but still sizable in acreage. It's a great place to get in some fishing and hunting. Or you can enjoy the wildlife."

Ethan saw them out, then locked up the office behind them.

As Isabella and J.R. headed for his pickup, she said, "I know this is the best place for Baron right now, but it doesn't feel right going home without him."

Home? The word had rolled off her tongue, but rather than own up to the slip, she let it slide, hoping J.R. hadn't noticed.

It was an easy mistake, she told herself. She'd stayed at the ranch over the weekend and had easily settled in. Too easily, actually, since J.R.'s ranch would never be home to her.

He opened the passenger-side door for her, and she slid into the seat. As he circled the pickup and got behind the wheel, she glanced down at her blouse, at the smudge of dirt and blood. The garment was new, and the stain probably wouldn't come out, but it didn't really matter. She was glad that Baron would be okay.

"Thank goodness we didn't have to put him down," J.R. said. "I was afraid that's what Ethan was going to recommend, and it would have been a tough decision to make."

Isabella knew just what J.R. meant. Losing that puppy would have been sad. Yet ranchers had to face the harsh realities whenever animals were seriously injured or sick. Putting an animal out of its misery was a fact of life for them, something they took in stride.

And that, she realized, was one more reason to believe that J.R. was a city slicker at heart.

Before he knew it, J.R. would grow tired of ranching and head back to Los Angeles—where he belonged.

The drive home was quiet, and even though J.R. and Isabella were both relieved to know that Baron would pull through, they were sorry to leave the puppy behind.

By the time they arrived back at the ranch, it was getting dark.

"Well," Isabella said as J.R. parked the pickup and shut off the ignition, "I'd better get inside and check out the plaster."

"Aren't you hungry?" he asked.

"Actually, I worked through lunch, so I'm starved."

As J.R. led Isabella to the door, he couldn't help thinking about the way she'd jumped right in when Baron got hurt, going the extra distance. She was becoming a part of the ranch. She belonged here; she just hadn't realized it yet.

When they entered the house, they found Frank and Toby waiting in the kitchen with Evie.

Toby, who'd been leaning against the refrigerator, pushed off and crossed the room to meet them, his face a mask of worry. "How's Baron? Is he…? Did he…?"

"He's going to be fine," J.R. said. "Dr. Eldridge just wanted him to stay overnight for observation."

"I never should have kept him with me." Toby's blue

eyes glistened with regret. "It's my fault that he got hurt. And I want you to know how sorry I am."

"Hey," J.R. said. "Baron is just a puppy, but he's a cattle dog. There's a lot he needs to learn. And I suspect he'll know better than to get too close to a horse's hooves from now on."

"We held off on eating dinner until you got back," Evie said. "Everything is still warm, so if you'll give me a minute or two, I'll get it on the table."

"Do you need any help?" Frank asked her.

J.R. shot a glance at his foreman. What had provoked him to make an offer like that? Not that J.R. didn't appreciate the fact that Frank was being polite, it just seemed...well, odd, that's all.

"Thanks," Evie told the cowboy. "I've got it all under control."

As she grabbed two pot holders and carried a ceramic baking dish toward the dining room, Frank watched her go, his interest in the cook going a bit above and beyond.

True to her word, Evie had the food on the table in a matter of minutes. And before long, the five of them dined on meat loaf, baked potatoes and a garden salad with buttermilk ranch dressing.

Evie might be a fabulous cook, and Isabella might assume that J.R.'s relationship with her was strictly business—that of employer/employee—but that wasn't the case. Before Isabella's weekend visit, Evie and J.R. had eaten all their meals together. But when the older woman had concluded that J.R. had romance on his mind, she'd made sure that he and Isabella had eaten in private.

Now that J.R. had begun hiring ranch hands, everyone would eat together.

Still, J.R. looked forward to getting Isabella alone again in the courtyard one day soon. He envisioned a quiet, romantic dinner for two. When he was able to pull that off, he would go all out with candles, music, wine…

"This is the best meat loaf I've had in ages," Frank said, lifting his napkin and blotting his mouth. "You're a great cook."

Evie, whose cheeks bore a natural rosy hue, flushed a deeper shade of pink. "Thank you, Frank. It's fun to cook for people who enjoy eating."

J.R. leaned back in his seat, watching as the cook and the foreman snuck glances at each other. There was something simmering between the two, and it was kind of nice to see.

He didn't know much about Frank, just that the man had lost his wife to cancer about fifteen or twenty years ago and had never remarried. He'd had to raise Toby, their only child, alone. So, for that reason, the father and son were especially close.

J.R. couldn't help but feel as though he needed to watch over Evie, to make sure she didn't get hurt. She'd been devastated when she lost her husband, and even more so when her stepchildren had all but shut her out of their lives. And the kindhearted woman didn't need any more disappointments.

Frank seemed like a reliable guy, though, and the references he'd provided had checked out. J.R. also prided himself on being a good judge of character, and both Frank and his son clearly were men of exemplary character.

As J.R. glanced across the table, catching Isabella's eye, he tossed her a smile. He'd trusted his instincts with Isabella, too. And hers was a sterling character, as well, wrapped in a bright whirl of Southwestern colors.

When they'd all finished dinner, Evie excused herself and went to bring out dessert—big slices of double-fudge cake that had them all oohing and aahing.

"You're going to have to roll me out of here," Isabella said, clearly joking about how good the cake was.

But J.R. had no intention of her rolling anywhere, other than into his bed, which was obviously not going to happen anytime soon.

As Evie began to pick up the dessert plates, and Frank jumped in to help, J.R. said, "Now might be a good time to check out the plaster work."

"You'll see that the crew got a lot done today," Evie said, pausing in the doorway that led to the kitchen. "But they didn't finish. This room is just one of several they'll have to plaster tomorrow."

After the table was cleared, Toby and Frank excused themselves to go to the bunkhouse, and J.R. and Isabella began a slow tour of the house, checking out the walls.

The new application of plaster looked good to him, although he wasn't entirely sold on the adobe brick that showed through in spots.

"What do you think?" he asked.

"They did a nice job." Isabella carefully studied the walls and the texture. "This is exactly what I asked them to do."

As they entered the guestroom in which Isabella had

slept, a room he thought of as hers, they continued to study the workmanship.

Rather, *she* continued to peruse the room. He was more intent on studying her.

As she reached the foot of the bed, she placed her hand on the comforter and turned toward the vase, where the roses had fully bloomed.

"Are Frank and Toby the first hands you've hired?"

"Yes."

"Where did you find them?"

He wasn't sure why she'd asked, why she cared, but he had no reason to keep it a secret. "Toby answered an ad I placed in the paper. And during our interview, he mentioned that his father was out of work. I asked to meet with him, too. Why?"

"It's just the mother hen in me, I suppose." She fingered the top of the antique dresser. "Frank seemed... Well, I got the feeling that he was interested in Evie. Maybe even romantically."

So J.R. hadn't been the only one to catch the I'm-sweet-on-you glances. "I noticed that, too."

"It's really touching," Isabella said. "I mean, assuming the interest is mutual."

So Isabella *did* have a romantic side. Otherwise, she wouldn't be impressed by Frank's interest in Evie. That was a good sign, J.R. supposed.

"I conducted a pretty thorough background check on both men, so if you're concerned about Evie, I think it's fair to say that she'd be in good hands if anything developed between them."

Was that it? Was Isabella concerned that she wouldn't be in good hands with J.R.?

As their gazes met, something hot and fluid rushed between them, something even she would be hard-pressed to ignore or to downplay.

He cupped her cheek with one hand, and his thumb caressed her skin. He continued to take in every bit of her pretty face, yet in his peripheral vision, he spotted the bed in the background, the goose-down comforter that promised to be a lot softer than a grassy field.

What he wouldn't give to take her in his arms, to kiss her senseless. To lay her on that bed and make love to her until dawn.

She stepped back, breaking the mesmerizing spell that seemed to hold them both captive.

He spotted the hesitation in her eyes, a sign that she was questioning her desire for him. But he wouldn't push. Not yet.

"I really need to get to bed," she said, taking a step back. "I have a meeting tomorrow morning with a guy who wants to display my blankets and tapestries in his stores, so I'll be leaving early for that. And then, in the evening, I have to attend my step-sister's birthday party. So I won't be able to stay here tomorrow night. I hope you're okay with that."

Actually, he wasn't okay with it. He had a feeling she was trying to put some distance between them, and he wanted her to stay at the ranch, like she'd agreed to. But she had a job to do, a career to build. And family was important.

"I understand," he said. "Will you be back on Wednesday?"

"Yes, of course. We have an agreement." She took another step back, her gaze still on him. "You're right, you know."

"Right about what?"

"When you said that staying here, sleeping under your roof, would provide me with a better perception of the house. It's working."

So she wasn't running scared? She was actually looking forward to coming back to the ranch?

Her body language wasn't very convincing, though. Yet her eager response to his kiss and the passion that simmered in her eyes was.

Isabella Mendoza was a contradiction—a lovely one, and J.R. couldn't seem to get enough of her.

"I'm afraid you won't see much of me over the next few days," she added. "I have a lot to do to get ready for Fiesta. Opening day is on the sixteenth."

"When does the art show begin?"

"On the sixteenth. But even if it didn't, I wouldn't miss opening day for anything."

Oh, yeah?

Then neither would J.R.

Chapter Seven

Opening day of Fiesta was always exciting. The festivities officially began at nine o'clock in front of the Alamo, with singing, dancing and pageantry.

One of the highlights was the cutting off of an official's necktie to signify the casual dress and the party atmosphere for the next ten days of the festival. But nothing was more exciting than the breaking of the *cascarones* as the crowd proclaimed *"Viva Fiesta!"*

Cascarones, Isabella had learned when she moved back to San Antonio as an adult, was a Mexican tradition. At various celebrations, people broke decorated, confetti-filled eggshells over the heads of friends and loved ones for good luck and good cheer.

So, two days ago, Isabella and Sarah had made a dozen of them. First, they poked two small holes at each end. Then they blew on one side, forcing the egg white and the yolk out the other. Afterward, they rinsed them out. When the eggs had dried thoroughly, they decorated each shell with bright paint and glitter. Next, using a paper funnel, they filled the shells with confetti and sealed the hole shut with a piece of tissue and glue.

Isabella would never forget the first time she'd witnessed the opening day ceremony and the breaking of the *cascarones*. She'd been in awe of the military band, the flamenco dancers, the mariachis—the sheer pageantry of it all. She hadn't wanted to miss a single exhibit, program or presentation.

She'd admired the local artists who'd exhibited their work—the incredible paintings, miniatures, pottery and other crafts. She'd eagerly looked forward to the next Fiesta, so she could show off her blankets and tapestries, too.

Her only regret had been that she'd missed out on so many Fiestas during the years she'd lived in California.

As she and Sarah stood in the center of the plaza, holding a basket filled with their colorful *cascarones,* she couldn't quell her excitement.

She'd dressed for the occasion in a bright, Southwestern skirt and a matching red blouse. She also wore some of the silver jewelry she'd purchased at last year's Fiesta.

"Good morning," a male voice boomed over the din of the crowd.

Isabella turned to see J.R. heading her way, with Toby at his side. Toby had dressed the part of the cowboy he truly was, but her focus was on the wannabe rancher.

J.R. looked sharp in his new boots and Stetson,

although she suspected he'd be more at home in tailor-made suits and designer shoes. Still, she couldn't help casting a lingering gaze his way.

As he closed the gap between them, she ignored her rising pulse rate and asked about Baron.

"Other than the stitches on his head, you'd never know he'd had a run-in with a horse."

"That's good." She offered him a smile, yet struggled with the excitement she felt at seeing him again.

J.R.'s presence always set her senses on edge. At least, that's the excuse she made for the buzz that rippled through her when she saw him approach.

Since she'd finished out the week at Molly's Pride, she'd returned a time or two to check up on the workers and to line them out, but she hadn't been able to devote the time she'd wanted to spend on his project. A part of her wanted to move back into his guestroom so she could oversee the progress of the workers. J.R. had been right about living there in the midst of the renovations. It had given her a better perspective.

"How are things going?" she asked. "Has the tile man finished yet?"

"Yes. The fountain is now full of water and in good working condition."

"I can't wait to see it." And if truth be told, she couldn't wait to return to the ranch, to roll up her sleeves and get busy renovating and decorating the old hacienda. "What about the electrician? Did he finish wiring for the stereo?"

"He sure did. And as you suggested, I purchased some hanging plants that hide the speakers completely.

The courtyard is really coming together. When Fiesta is over I'd like you to join me for dinner. You'll be surprised by the difference."

Since they'd been skating around that kiss for the past two weeks, she really should nix anything even remotely romantic, like a dinner in his courtyard. But her enthusiasm for the project and her curiosity got the better of her. Besides, she had her heart under control now. The preparation for Fiesta had provided a nice buffer. "I'd love to see it."

The announcer called out, drawing their attention to the festivities.

"Last year was the first time I ever attended Fiesta," J.R. said. "But I missed opening day."

"Well, you're just in time for the breaking of the *cascarones*." She proceeded to explain the history behind them, as well as the meaning. She lifted her basket, showing him the ones she and Sarah had made. "We have extras in case we run into someone who doesn't have any."

Toby, who stood to J.R.'s left, kept sneaking glances at Sarah, whose lightly freckled cheeks bore a faint flush that suggested she was all too aware of his interest in her.

Sensing their shyness and curiosity, Isabella made the introductions.

"Sarah is my assistant," she added.

Toby lifted his hat respectfully, and the petite redhead flushed an even deeper shade of pink.

There was something about a cowboy that appealed to a lot of women, Isabella thought. And she had to admit that she was no different. But try as he might, J.R. just wasn't the real McCoy.

Too bad, she thought. She almost wished that he were.

As the crowd began to smash *cascarones* on the heads of friends and loved ones, Isabella reached into her basket and chose a red egg. She lifted it toward J.R. "You might want to remove that fancy hat."

"Why?" he asked.

"Because I'm going to officially wish you good luck and good cheer."

J.R. did as she asked, and rising up on tiptoe, she broke the egg against his head, baptizing him with confetti.

"Viva Fiesta!" she shouted.

He grinned, oblivious to the colorful sprinkles of paper littering his blond hair and forehead. "Thanks for the good wishes." He glanced at the eggs in her basket. "You said that you brought extras. Can you spare one of those?"

"Of course." She watched as he chose a blue egg with red and yellow zigzags down the middle. Then he broke it on top her head.

"Viva Fiesta!" he said.

Isabella pegged Sarah with an egg, then took another and gave Toby the same chance to remove his hat as she'd given J.R.

The young man, with his short-cropped, wheat-colored hair, wasn't exactly what you'd call handsome, but he was pleasant-looking. And he had a polite way about him.

Sarah, it seemed, had noticed that, too.

Isabella was glad. Interest in a new man would be a welcome diversion and just might help to heal her broken heart.

"Did you set up your blankets and tapestries in the same spot as last year?" J.R. asked.

"Pretty close," she said. "My dad volunteered to sit with my exhibit. He knows how much the opening ceremony means to me and encouraged me to take part. But since he plays in a band and needs to meet with the other musicians, I have to get back to relieve him."

"If it's okay with you," J.R. said, "I'd like to see what you've made this year. I'm sure I could use one or two at the house."

"I'll show you what I have." She led the way to her exhibit. "But you might find something you like better from one of the other artisans, so don't feel obligated to purchase one of mine."

When they reached the booth where Luis Mendoza waited, J.R. reached out his hand in greeting to José Mendoza's cousin. "It's good to see you again."

"How have you been?" Luis asked, taking J.R.'s hand and giving it a firm shake. "Busy with the new ranch, I suspect. I'd like to see it some time. Isabella told me it's really going to be something when you finish renovating and redecorating the house."

"You're welcome to stop by anytime," J.R. said.

The men chatted a while, then Isabella's father excused himself to find the other members of his mariachi band.

As J.R. looked at the tapestry Isabella had created during the winter months, he fingered it gently. "This is beautiful."

"I'm glad you like it."

"It would look nice hanging in the great room."

She smiled, pleased that he thought so, too. "I'll put it away so no one thinks it's for sale."

While she folded the tapestry he liked, J.R. perused her blankets. As he did, she watched his movements, his facial expressions. His words and tone indicated sincerity, yet she was still wary of him, just as she would be with any of the tourists who found her traditions "quaint."

She checked her emotions each time she felt herself drawn to his one-dimpled grin, melting a little when he glanced her way.

One day, she reminded herself for the umpteenth time, J.R. would grow tired of playing cowboy and go back to his sophisticated lifestyle in Los Angeles. So why let down her guard when she ought to be raising it? Why even consider getting involved with him any more than she already had?

Focus on the list, she told herself. Listen to logic, not your heart. Don't grow weak just because of that kiss in the grass.

She'd had a good reason for making a list of qualities for a perfect mate in the first place, so she took the time now to consider each trait she was looking for.

Someone down to earth with a steady job.

That was important, and Isabella didn't care what Jane had said. Leaving a lucrative career and moving halfway across the country to try his hand at something he'd never done before wasn't a sign of someone dependable and solid.

Someone sensitive and caring.

Okay, so J.R. had displayed a tender heart, especially when it came to Baron.

Someone able to make a commitment.

Come on, now. What made her think he'd settle down with her, when he'd obviously had countless women in the past, none of whom had rocked his single world enough to make him consider marriage?

A guy with a good sense of humor.

She again thought of the day they'd fallen into each other's arms on the grass, how they'd laughed over the mishap. Then he'd kissed her until she'd nearly melted right into the field of wildflowers.

True, their chemistry couldn't be discounted. Her vivid memories of a heated kiss proved that.

She also had to admit that J.R. was handsome, but looks weren't a top priority for her. The most important thing of all was that she could fall deeply and madly in love with a man, trusting that he would love her back, just as much. She wanted and needed someone who wasn't afraid of the teamwork it would take to make a marriage last.

A giggle erupted, and Isabella stopped her musing long enough to see that Sarah and Toby had managed to push through that awkward stage and had moved on to innocent flirtation.

Her gaze returned to J.R., who'd also caught the flushed cheeks, giggles and shy smiles.

He stepped closer to Isabella and whispered, "For the record, Toby's a good kid."

"So is Sarah."

They were talking about the younger couple, yet their gazes locked on each other. That heart-thumping, soul-stirring rush that rose up whenever their eyes met surged again—this time stronger than ever.

"Romance is definitely in the air," J.R. said, apparently alluding to Frank and Evie, and now Toby and Sarah.

Isabella just hoped it wasn't contagious.

For the next few days, Isabella found her resolve to avoid J.R. slowly weakening. Each morning, he showed up at Fiesta, bringing her coffee—just the way she liked it—and a muffin or a sweet roll.

"I thought you needed to be at the ranch," she'd said yesterday, as she took the blueberry scone he'd handed her.

"Frank is a natural-born cattleman with years of experience. He'll be okay without me for a while."

"Still," Isabella said, "I'm surprised you're back again."

"Don't be. There's an artist down the way who works with metal. I like some of the sculptures he's created, and he told me he had the perfect piece for me. He promised to bring it from home today. If I like it—and I have a feeling I will—I'm going to buy it."

Twenty minutes later, J.R. returned with a rustic sculpture made of barbed wire, spurs and who knew what else—the key to a John Deere tractor perhaps?

"What are you going to do with that?" she'd asked.

"I thought it would look great in my office."

She'd crossed her arms and arched a skeptical brow. As it was, the furniture in that one particular room was modern, and all the equipment—the fax, the copier, the computer—was state-of-the-art. Of course, she couldn't very well expect him to go back to the stone age in that respect. And she supposed he ought to be able to do whatever he wanted in the office.

"Interesting," she said, knowing she would never have a piece like that in her house.

The next morning, as she went up on tiptoe, trying to hang up one of her favorite tapestries in the front of her exhibit, she heard J.R.'s voice as he approached.

"Come on," he said. "This is going to be a lot easier on you if you try to keep up."

Who was he talking to? A small child? She glanced over her shoulder and saw that he had Baron on a leash. Other than a shaved spot on the head where Dr. Eldridge had sutured his wound, the puppy appeared to have completely recovered from his run-in with Ol' Smokey.

Isabella set the tapestry back on the table, then went to greet the rascally pup. She knelt on the ground and scratched his head. "Hey, buddy. How're you doing?"

He wiggled, and his tail wagged like crazy, as he gave her a hearty and affectionate lick.

J.R., who was juggling a small white paper sack and a cardboard carrier that held what appeared to be hot coffee, dropped the leash beside her. "Can you hold onto him while I set this down?"

"I'd be glad to." Isabella took the strap in hand, then glanced up at J.R. and smiled. "He looks great."

"He sure does." J.R. placed the box and the sack on the table.

Isabella had begun to expect J.R. to stop by with treats, so she'd gone without breakfast this morning. "What did you pick up this time?"

"Churros." He handed her a heat-insulated cup of coffee, which he'd again prepared with a splash of cream and sweetener.

"You're going to spoil me," she said.

He tossed her a bright-eyed grin, which made her wonder if that had been his plan all along. Then he reached into the sack, pulled out one of the doughnut-like treats and offered it to her.

She took it, noting that it was still warm from the vendor's stove. "I love these things."

"Me, too."

The guy had been racking up points, whether that was his intention or not, and she couldn't help but lower her guard just a bit.

He hadn't been coming on strong at all, which is what she'd expected. As a result, she was growing more comfortable in his presence, knowing that she was in full control.

If he asked her out, maybe it wouldn't hurt to agree. It's not as if she had to sleep with him.

Of course, he was a wonderful kisser, which meant his lovemaking skills were probably amazing. And it had been so long since she'd…

J.R. took a sip of his coffee, then scanned the immediate area. "Where's Sarah?"

"Fussing with her hair and lipstick." Isabella smiled. "Did you know that Toby asked her out? And that he's meeting her here today?"

"Yes. That's why we came in separate cars. He's taking her to the Fiesta carnival at the Alamodome."

An actual date, Isabella thought. How long had it been since she'd gone out with a guy she found attractive?

Too long, she decided.

A day at the carnival sounded like a lot of fun. Too bad

she had to man her exhibit. Still, if Sarah watched it for her one day, she might be able to steal an afternoon away.

Isabella slid a glance at J.R., then scolded herself for letting her thoughts stray. He probably wasn't the Tilt-a-Whirl type anyway. Still, if he asked…?

She just might say yes.

When he didn't, she banished her silly romantic fantasies by bringing up their decorating project and the renovations to his house. "By the way, I have pictures of the furniture I'd like your permission to purchase and sample fabric for the window coverings."

"When did you find time for that?"

"Last night. The design center I normally use stayed open late for me." She bit into her churro and savored the sugar-and-cinnamon taste of the deep-fried treat.

J.R. took another sip of coffee. "I've been busy in the evenings, too. Last night, I ordered a fifty-two-inch plasma TV."

Before she could comment or question where he planned to put a television that massive, Sarah arrived, her hair combed and curled. Mascara enhanced her eyes, and a light coat of blush covered her freckled cheeks. The young woman looked prettier than Isabella had ever seen her—happier, too.

When was the last time Isabella had fussed over a man? When had she experienced the excitement of a special date?

"You look great," Isabella told Sarah.

"Thanks." The younger woman beamed.

Had J.R. not been standing there, the two might have

lapsed into typical girl talk: Is there too much curl in my hair? Do these jeans make my butt look big?

As it was, they turned toward the crowd perusing the art exhibits, noting a boy and a girl who were carrying a cardboard box as they approached Isabella's booth.

"What do you have there?" J.R. asked.

"They're kittens," the boys said. "Four of them. Me and my sister found them. Their mom got hit by a car, so we took 'em home. Our dad said we could have one, but we have to get rid of the rest."

Isabella handed Baron's leash back to J.R. so she could get a better look. She reached for an orange tabby, picked it up and drew it to her cheek. She'd always wanted a pet and had seriously considered getting one to keep her company. Since she didn't particularly like living alone, she thought a watchdog might be a good idea. But dogs needed a lot of care.

Cats, on the other hand, didn't require as much time. Should she consider a kitten?

"They're really cute," Sarah said. "How much do you want for them?"

"Aw, heck," the boy said. "We don't want to make money on 'em, lady. We just want to find them good homes."

Sarah eased closer to Isabella and studied the little orange tabby she was cuddling. "Maybe you should treat yourself to an early birthday present."

Should she?

"When is your birthday?" J.R. asked.

Isabella pondered her response. To be honest, she

was struggling a bit over turning thirty and wanted the day to pass quietly, without any fanfare.

"Is it a secret?" he asked.

"No. As far as I'm concerned, it's just another day." And it was. She didn't want him to get any ideas. If he bought her a present, it would make their relationship even more…awkward than it already was. "For the record, it's on the twenty-third."

"But it's not an ordinary day," Sarah said. "It's one of the biggies, and I think you should celebrate."

Isabella gave her a please-don't-even-go-there look, although it was too late. She could already see the wheels and cogs turning in J.R.'s head.

J.R. couldn't help smiling at Isabella's discomfort over her upcoming birthday. At least, the age thing was his best guess.

If the birthday was a "biggie," she was probably turning thirty. Apparently, that bothered her, but he couldn't see why it would.

"Don't stress about getting older," he said. "You're still a *pollo primavera*."

She scrunched her face at his attempt at Spanish and laughed. "Are you trying to call me a *spring chicken?*"

"Did I say it wrong?"

She laughed. "I'm not fluent in Spanish by any means, but I think that's one of the idioms that doesn't translate very well."

Suddenly realizing the two kids were waiting for her to make a decision, she slowly turned and reluctantly placed the kitten back in the box. "I'm sorry, you guys.

As sweet as this little thing is and as much as I'd love to take it home with me, I can't."

She crossed her arms and watched the kids walk away, their shoulders slumped.

Isabella's seemed to slump a bit, too.

"Why didn't you take the cat?" he asked.

"Because I live in a small apartment, not on a ranch." Her gaze followed the children, her expression almost wistful. "Besides, I need a pet like I need a hole in the head."

He'd seen her with Baron, seen the way the pup had taken to her, too. The puppy had followed her through the house, and when she'd worked on her loom, he'd curled up at her feet, just wanting to be near her.

"Why don't you think you need a pet?" he asked.

"They require time and attention, and I'm very busy." She shrugged a single shoulder. "But the kitten was cute, wasn't it?"

J.R. was actually a dog person, but he supposed that little orange tabby was okay—for a cat.

Sarah broke into a grin, and when J.R. looked up and saw Toby approach, he realized why.

While he didn't envy the young couple their nervousness, he did envy their excitement and the newness of a budding romance.

"Hey," Toby said.

Sarah glanced down at the ground. When she looked up and smiled, her cheeks bore a rosy tint. "Hi."

"Are you ready to go?" he asked.

"I guess so." She glanced at Isabella, then at J.R and back to Toby. "I mean, yes. I'm ready."

"Have fun," Isabella said.

As the couple walked away, it took everything J.R. had not to slip his hand into Isabella's, to draw her to his side. To tell her that he wanted to go to the carnival, too. That not only did he want to work with her on the renovations of the house, but he also wanted to play and have fun with her.

But he couldn't very well admit that yet. Not when she'd made it clear that she wasn't ready.

Of course, he sensed that her resolve was weakening. It wouldn't be much longer.

She turned to him, her lips parted.

Damn, she was a beautiful woman. And he realized that a lot of what he'd done since the beginning of the year had been done, in large part, because of her.

Sure, he'd wanted a ranch of his own for years. And he was glad he'd made the purchase, no matter how this thing with Isabella turned out.

But the actual move, relocating to Texas from California, had also been motivated, at least in part, by his desire to be close to her. He'd wanted to pursue a relationship with her that wouldn't leave them at a disadvantage because of the distance between them.

J.R. considered himself a patient man, but that patience was wearing thin and he was ready to put more of his plan into action.

If Isabella was still reluctant about their becoming romantically involved, he'd just wear her down.

He was used to getting what he wanted—and he wanted her. The more he'd gotten to know her, the more he was convinced that she was the woman for him.

"Well," he said, giving Baron's leash a gentle tug. "I need to go. I've got a few things to take care of while I'm in town."

Before he could walk away, an elderly couple wandering through the exhibits stopped to look at one of the blankets Isabella had displayed.

"See, honey?" the silver-haired woman said. "This is the one I told you about. I love the colors and the design."

The man reached for his credit card.

As Baron got to his feet and lunged forward, tugging on the leash, J.R. said, "I'll leave you to your customers."

"Okay. Thanks for the coffee and churros. I'll see you tomorrow."

The fact that she'd come to expect him was a good sign, and a smile stretched across his face.

As soon as he was out of her sight, he reached for his cell phone and asked the operator to patch him through to Red. When someone answered, he asked to speak to either José or Maria Mendoza.

Maria's voice came over the line as she introduced herself. "How can I help?"

"This is J.R., Maria. I'd like to reserve your back room for a birthday party on the twenty-third. It's a surprise."

After checking the date, Maria came back on the line and told him he was in luck. The room was available.

"How many people are you expecting?" she asked.

"Well, the dinner party is to celebrate Isabella's thirtieth birthday, so I'll be including the Mendozas and the Fortunes."

They chatted for a moment or two about the menu, then Maria asked if he had any special requests.

"Actually," he admitted. "I have several."

He went on to explain what he wanted and let her know to add it to his bill.

When the call ended and he put away his cell phone, he and Baron moved through the throng of Fiesta shoppers, as he looked for the kids peddling the kittens.

Hopefully, the orange tabby was still available.

J.R. glanced at the pup. "You aren't going to give that little cat a hard time, are you?"

He hoped not. Because if he had his way, Isabella and the kitten would be happily moving into the ranch before the month's end.

Chapter Eight

On the day of Isabella's party, J.R. arrived at the restaurant early, just to make sure everything was on track. The florist had come through, bringing a bouquet of red roses for each table. And everything else had been set up just as he'd ordered—food, music, entertainment.

As he made his way through the throng of family and friends, he greeted each of them, welcoming them and thanking them for coming.

He was glad to see how many had showed up, although certainly not as many as on New Year's Eve, when everyone had been in town for the holidays. His father was here, sitting next to Uncle Patrick and Aunt Lacey. J.R. had hoped Aunt Lily would make it, but she'd been feeling under the weather and had remained at the Double Crown.

From what he'd heard, his aunt, Cindy Fortune, was

back in town, but he hadn't extended a personal invitation to her. If she showed up at the restaurant, so be it. But if not, he certainly wouldn't be disappointed.

Cindy had always been a wild child. As a young woman, she'd run off and had become a showgirl, something that had been an embarrassment for the family. And in the course of her life, she was married four times, although none of the unions had lasted. She had managed to have four children, two with her second husband, and one each with husbands three and four.

Her kids, J.R.'s cousins, had turned out pretty well, considering the various upheavals in their lives that had been caused by their mother's flair for the dramatic.

Cindy's only daughter, Frannie, was here—alone. Apparently, Josh, her seventeen-year-old son, was on a date with his steady girlfriend tonight. There was no telling where Frannie's husband, Lloyd Fredericks, was, and J.R. didn't ask. Instead, he gave the lovely, stylishly dressed blonde a hug.

"It's good to see you," he told his cousin. And it was, but it was also sad to note how subdued the once fun-loving and spirited woman had grown over the years.

"I haven't had a chance to welcome you to Red Rock," Frannie said. "I'm glad you made the move."

After a little small talk, J.R. went on to greet the other guests.

The Red Rock Mendozas were here—Maria and José, of course, and four of their five children, nearly all of whom were either married or engaged. Roberto, who lived in Denver, was the only one who'd been unable to attend.

Isabella's four half siblings were here, and J.R. made a point of thanking each of them for coming.

As he continued to make the rounds, he stopped to chat briefly with Jorge Mendoza and Jane Gilliam. Jane was a friend of Isabella's, and Jorge was a cousin of hers. The happy couple were looking forward to their wedding next month.

J.R.'s brother Darr arrived with his fiancée, Bethany.

"How's it going?" J.R. asked Darr.

His brother slipped an arm around a very pregnant Bethany and drew her close. "Great. How about you?"

"So far, so good." J.R. slid him a slow smile. After this evening, he hoped to be able to proclaim his complete happiness, too.

Nicholas, another one of J.R.'s brothers, was here with Charlene London, his future wife.

Damn, J.R. thought. Romantic relationships were springing up all over Red Rock. Hopefully, he would find that romance was also in the cards for him and Isabella.

Their relationship had grown since opening day of Fiesta, although he hadn't tried to kiss her again.

He did, however, plan to make up for that tonight, when the crowd dissipated and they were alone. So, needless to say, he was looking forward to her arrival and to getting the party underway.

Initially, he'd thought about bringing her himself, once the guests had gathered. But he'd worried that she might turn down his offer to take her to Red for dinner. So Luis, her father, had been assigned to get her to the restaurant at seven.

She would be expecting a quiet evening with her

father, but she was in for a big surprise. She'd also be wearing red—if she agreed to the request Luis had made on J.R.'s behalf.

It was all part of J.R.'s master plan, although the birthday party had been an unexpected twist.

Things were certainly falling into place—the party, their budding relationship.

"She's coming!" someone called from the doorway.

The guests grew still, awaiting her arrival.

J.R.'s pulse pounded with anticipation, although party excitement had nothing to do with it. He always found his senses on high alert whenever Isabella entered a room.

As she swept through the doorway wearing a bright red dress, complementing her womanly curves, he studied her in rapt silence as those around him shouted, "Surprise!"

Her lips parted, and her eyes widened as she took in her surroundings and realized that someone had planned a party and that she was the guest of honor.

She looked at her father, who was smiling broadly.

"Who…planned all this?" she asked, her pretty brow furrowed.

Luis pointed to J.R., who took that moment to close the gap between them.

"Are you surprised?" he asked.

"Floored is more like it."

There wasn't time for any additional chitchat because her friends and family began to swarm around her, wishing her a happy birthday.

J.R. stepped back, allowing this portion of the evening to be hers alone.

As the party wound down, he would steal a few moments of his own.

Isabella couldn't believe all the trouble J.R. must have gone to in an effort to surprise her, and while she hadn't wanted any of the usual birthday fanfare, she couldn't help feeling both happy and honored that he'd pulled it all together—and in such a short time.

From the first day she'd returned to Red Rock to visit the Mendoza side of the family, she'd been welcomed with open arms. And tonight she'd felt even more loved, more accepted.

She greeted her family and friends, thanking each one for coming. She paused when J.R.'s voice came over a microphone.

"Excuse me," he said. "Can I have your attention?"

Isabella turned and faced the center of the room where the handsome rancher stood next to a portable dance floor, a mike in hand. For some reason, dressed in black jeans and a Western jacket, a white shirt and bolo tie, he didn't look at all like a city slicker tonight.

A hush fell over the crowd, as they waited for him to continue.

"I'd like to thank you all for coming this evening and sharing in a very special occasion—Isabella Mendoza's birthday. As part of the welcome, I'd like to invite her brother, Javier Mendoza, to sing a song to this very special lady. If I had the talent and the voice that Javier has, I'd be singing those words myself, each one from my heart."

Isabella's oldest half brother made his way to the

center of the room, stepped behind the keyboard and adjusted the microphone. Then he began to play and sing "Lady in Red."

It was Javier's voice singing the words, but as Isabella sought J.R., as their gazes met and locked, she realized that the lyrics were indeed coming from his heart.

As Javier continued to play and sing, J.R. approached Isabella and held out his hand.

Her heart flip-flopped in her chest, yet she let him lead her to the dance floor.

At this very moment, any reservations she'd ever had about him—about *them*—flew by the wayside as she stepped into his arms and began to sway to the music. Tonight her heart took the lead.

J.R. might not consider himself a singer, but he definitely knew how to dance.

"I can't believe you did this for me," she said.

He drew her closer. "Like Sarah said, this birthday is a biggie, Isabella. I thought you ought to have a proper celebration."

Charmed by his thoughtfulness and more than a little enamored with the romantic gesture of the song, Isabella leaned into him, relishing the feel of his arms around her, the beat of his heart against hers.

As they continued to move to the sexy beat of the music, she savored the musky scent of his aftershave and the feel of his cheek against hers.

When the last note ended, when the song was through, a rousing cheer erupted, followed by claps and whistles.

"Enjoy the evening and your guests," J.R. said, releasing her from his embrace. "I'll talk to you later."

As he turned and walked away, her knees wobbled. She hadn't realized how much she'd depended on his body as support, but she did her best to shake off the effects of their arousing embrace.

Ten minutes later, dinner was served in the main dining room, where red roses graced each linen-draped, candlelit table. Isabella had assumed that J.R. would sit with her, but he chose another seat, leaving her to be with her father and siblings.

What was with that?

The contradiction unbalanced her. Was he giving her space? Respecting her wishes not to get involved with him? Or had she been misreading his interest all along?

Yet throughout the night, his eyes were always on her, and she found herself constantly wondering where he was, what he was doing.

After dinner, she was lavished with cards and gifts— a bottle of wine, a basket of soaps and lotions, a CD of her favorite Tejana music—and she thanked everyone for their kindness and generosity.

As chocolate cake was served, and the party began to wind down, J.R. finally approached her again. This time he carried a small, colorfully wrapped present with a fancy red bow.

"What's this?" she asked.

"A little something from me."

"You've done enough for me already." She swept her arm in Vanna White style, indicating the party. "You didn't need to get me a present."

"I know. But I wanted to. Open it."

She took the package and carefully removed the ribbon and paper. Then she lifted the lid and peered inside. On a piece of cotton sat an elegant, hand-crafted, silver-and-onyx necklace. She gasped at the beauty, the artwork. She pulled it out of the box, letting it dangle from the fingers of one hand as she fondled the black, glossy, inlaid gem with the other. "It's beautiful, J.R."

"It was handcrafted by one of the artisans at Fiesta. I saw it there the other day, and it reminded me of something you'd wear, something you'd like."

"I don't know what to say." The fact that he'd purchased something culturally appealing to her made her wonder if he really *did* understand where she was coming from. "Thank you."

"You're welcome." He took the piece from her and reached to unhook the clasp. "Here, let me."

She turned and drew the veil of her hair aside. As he placed the intricately designed necklace on her chest and drew the chain behind her neck, his hands lingered on her bare shoulders and sent a sizzle spiraling through her bloodstream. Her heart went topsy-turvy, as she fingered the black stone.

His hands slowly slid down her arms, and she struggled not to turn, to gaze into his eyes. She was losing the strength and the will to fight him off, to challenge the feelings that were growing by leaps and bounds.

She turned, and their eyes met. Something blazed between them—not only heat and arousal, but emotion as well—fusing them in an unexpected bond.

"I have something else for you," he said. "Come with me to my car."

"You've given me too much already," she said.

J.R. chuckled. "Don't thank me for this one, yet. You might insist that I keep it myself."

Curiosity urged her to follow.

As they strode through the restaurant and out the front door, she expected him to take her hand. In fact, if truth be told, she *wanted* him to.

But he didn't, and she fought off a wave of disappointment. Still she continued to walk by his side.

They headed toward his SUV, where Toby stood near the back end.

Toby hadn't been at the party. At least, she didn't remember seeing him. So what was he doing out here?

"What's going on?" she asked.

"Your other gift needed a sitter," J.R. said.

The explanation made no sense.

She watched Toby take a cardboard box from the back of the vehicle and pass it to J.R. Crossing her arms, she waited as he reached into the box and pulled out what appeared to be the same orange tabby kitten she'd seen at Fiesta.

He handed her the little ball of fur. "Take it home and see if you enjoy having a pet. If you think you can't take care of a kitten, let me know. I'll give it a home on the ranch."

"But I don't have any food for it," she said, stroking its little head.

"I've got everything you need right here—kitten chow, toys, a litter box."

Isabella cuddled the kitty, trying to decide whether she should accept J.R.'s gift or not.

"Is this the same kitten those kids had?" she asked.

He nodded. "I knew it was a struggle for you to give it back, which made me think you really wanted it. So I followed the kids and told them I'd take it. If I was wrong, and you're sure you don't want a cat, I'll take it home with me."

She wasn't sure if she should be impressed that he'd somehow sensed how badly she'd always wanted a pet, or angry that he'd been so presumptuous. Still, she continued to cuddle the kitten.

"I have to admit that she and Baron had their moments, but they seem to be getting used to each other now. So taking her back to the ranch won't be a big problem. But why don't you give it a try?"

She stroked the kitten again. "I worried about leaving a pet home all day while I worked. But I guess I can take her to the studio with me."

J.R. smiled then turned to his hired hand and nodded toward the white pickup that belonged to Isabella's father. "Toby, will you put the kitten supplies into the bed of that truck?"

"You got it, boss." Toby took a bigger box and a sack out of the back of J.R.'s vehicle, then did as he was instructed.

"Sarah's waiting inside," J.R. said.

Toby beamed before dashing into the restaurant.

As J.R. returned his attention to Isabella, that bond, that buzz—whatever it was that surged between them—was in overdrive.

In the light of a silvery moon, his thoughtfulness, as well as his musky, leathery scent turned her heart and her mind inside out. She no longer wanted to wait for him to make the first move.

She held the kitten to her chest with one hand and, with the other, reached up and cupped his cheek, felt the light bristle of his beard, the warmth of his skin.

Regret might rear its head tomorrow, or even later tonight, but that didn't matter right now. Mindful of the kitten, she drew his lips to hers and kissed him—softly, at first. But as their breaths mingled, as their tongues touched, the kiss deepened.

She'd never experienced desire like this before, and she feared she never would again.

If she were willing to let her body run rampant over her mind, if she could just set aside her list for a few hours…

Give in, something deep within her urged. *Let go.*

But she couldn't quite do that yet. Not tonight.

An important decision like that shouldn't be made in the heat of the moment. If she chose to have a sexual relationship with J.R., she wanted to do so with a clear head, and she definitely wasn't thinking rationally right now. So she released her hold and broke the kiss.

"I'd be more than happy to drive you home," he said, not indicating which home he was talking about—hers or his. And in a sense, it really didn't matter.

"I think it's best if I go with my father," she said.

"Are you sure?"

No, she wasn't. Did she dare consider dating a man whose lifestyle and culture were so different from her own?

She'd feel much better about all this if she made that decision in the morning light. "Can we talk more about this tomorrow?"

"Fair enough," he said. "I want you to be comfortable with whatever you decide. You call the shots."

Footsteps sounded as her father approached. "Am I interrupting anything?"

"No, Papa." Her fear of a relationship with J.R. had already done that.

"Good night," J.R. said. "I'll talk to you in the morning."

She thanked him again, then watched as he climbed into his SUV.

As she got into her father's pickup, she had an almost overwhelming compulsion to run back to J.R., to tell him she'd had a change of heart.

Instead she watched him leave.

As her father started the engine and began the drive back to San Antonio, she realized that she would be kicking herself all the way home.

J.R. returned to the restaurant long enough to pay the bill. He told José he'd continue to pick up the bar tab for those who remained, although he suspected that most of them had wound down and were ready to leave.

Once he'd gotten into the Escalade, he started the engine and turned on the radio. Then he began the drive back to the ranch.

He hadn't thought a kiss could be any better than the one he and Isabella had shared the day they'd picnicked, but he'd been wrong. If he'd ever had any doubts about

Isabella being the woman he wanted to spend the rest of his life with, they'd disappeared just minutes ago.

Things were coming together just the way he wanted them to. If he knew her as well as he thought he did, she was now ruing her decision to ride home with her father instead of him.

As a grin began to form, his cell phone rang.

For a moment, he wondered if it was her, calling him to tell him she'd changed her mind.

But it was his father's voice that sounded over the line. "Son, I meant to talk to you about something after Isabella's party, but you left before I got the chance."

"What's up?"

"Patrick and I were talking, and we think we should take a more active stance against those threats."

Concern overtook J.R.'s romantic thoughts. At least, for the moment. "What do you plan to do?"

"There's not a lot we *can* do until we find out who's making those threats and what they have against the Fortunes and the Mendozas. But Patrick and I have finally convinced Lily that she needs more protection on the Double Crown than just ranch hands. I'm on my way to tell Lily that I'm going to move in and stay with her until the culprit is caught."

J.R. was worried about his widowed aunt, too. When Uncle Ryan died four years ago of a brain tumor, Lily had been the love of his life. And now Lily was alone.

"To make matters worse," William said, "Cindy was involved in a car accident this afternoon."

Cindy Fortune had always marched to the beat of her own drummer. Divorced three times and widowed once, she'd never lacked a sexual relationship. Now seventy years old, with brassy blond hair and a flirtatious eye, she was still a fine-looking woman who could turn a man's head.

J.R. had never been too close to her, but then again, not many people in the family had been. Not only did she have a flair for the dramatic, she was also self-centered and, at times, self-destructive.

"What happened?" J.R. asked.

"Her car ran off the road."

"Was she badly injured?"

"From what I understand, she suffered a serious concussion and lacerations. She's been hospitalized, but she should pull through."

"I'm glad to hear that." J.R. wondered if alcohol had been involved.

"Here's the thing," his father said. "Neither Patrick nor I think it was an accident. Not with the arson fires and the threats we've been getting."

J.R. had to admit that his father had a point.

"I don't think anyone in the Fortune or the Mendoza family is entirely safe," his father added. "So keep an eye on Isabella. I realize that she's only a second cousin to the Red Rock Mendozas, but who knows what—or who—the guilty parties are really after."

If anything happened to Isabella, J.R. didn't know what he'd do, and the force of his emotion surprised him. "Don't worry, Dad. I'll look out for her."

J.R. slowed his vehicle until it came to a full stop. When it was safe, he made a U-turn and headed back to San Antonio.

He was going to look out for Isabella—whether she wanted him to or not.

At the same time, in a private hospital bed in Red Rock, pain exploded in Cindy Fortune's head, and she moaned. Her mind was a swirl of shadows and fog, and she struggled to sort through what had happened to her.

A car crash, she thought. That much she could piece together. And she'd been hurt. If the pain was any clue, her injuries were serious.

Oh, God, she thought, willing the sledgehammer in her brain to stop long enough for her to piece things together.

She'd returned to Red Rock in an attempt to reconcile with her only daughter. Of her four children, Frannie was the one she was closest to, although, if truth be told, they'd had a slew of problems and disagreements over the years.

They'd met for lunch today, and things had gone… Well, they hadn't gone all that well, but Frannie had at least seemed willing to give their mother-daughter relationship another chance.

But the car? The crash?

Oh, yes. It was coming back to her…

After leaving the restaurant, she'd been driving along, when, somehow, she'd lost control and had run off the road.

That's all she remembered, though—barreling through the guardrail and down an incline.

As she lay trapped in the driver's seat, she'd welcomed the loss of consciousness, because it had kept the pain at bay. And now she was in a hospital; she knew that much.

"Miss Fortune?" a male voice asked.

Cindy, who'd never kept the last names of any of her husbands, turned toward the sound and the blurred form of a man standing at her bedside, a man wearing a uniform and a badge.

"Yes?" she asked, blinking her eyes and trying to focus.

"Do you know anyone who might want to hurt you?" the officer asked.

Truthfully? In her seventy years on earth, she'd made the usual number of enemies along the way, but no one in particular came to mind. "Why do you ask?"

"Because your brakes have been tampered with."

Cindy tried to make sense of the shocking news. Was he suggesting that someone had tried to kill her?

The note she'd received a couple of months ago pressed through the clutter in her mind.

One of the Fortunes is not who you think, it had read.

She hadn't been the only one to receive that same cryptic message. Patrick and William, her brothers, had received similar, unsigned letters. And so had her sister-in-law, Lily.

To make matters more suspicious, there had been two different arson fires—first at Red, then at the Double Crown Ranch since then.

Try as she might, Cindy couldn't quite comprehend what had happened and what it might mean. Nor could she will herself to stay lucid long enough to tell the police officer that there could be a correlation.

As another wave of darkness rolled back and forth across her mind, as she drifted in and out of consciousness, she quit fighting to stay awake.

What was the use?

But as the fog briefly lifted, she had one lucid moment and was haunted by one irrefutable thought.

I deserve it, she told herself. *I deserve to be punished for what I did....*

Chapter Nine

"That was some party," Isabella's father said on the drive home. "It must have cost J.R. a small fortune. I didn't realize the two of you had gotten so close."

"It's complicated," Isabella said. But if the truth were known, she was now beginning to wonder if it was all very simple. Maybe she was the one who was complicating the issue by dragging her feet.

J.R. definitely cared for her. He was also very generous and thoughtful. And to top it all off, the chemistry between them was explosive.

So why was she riding home with her dad when she could have been with J.R.?

Fortunately, her father must have realized that she didn't want to go into detail because he didn't press for more.

Twenty minutes later, he dropped her off at her place, a small one-bedroom apartment located in a quiet San Antonio neighborhood. He helped her carry in all her gifts, including the kitten and the pet supplies J.R. had given her.

Then he kissed her goodnight and went home.

Now here she was, alone. Well, except for the kitten she'd decided to call Rusty.

She kicked off her shoes, plopped onto the sofa and watched Rusty check out his surroundings. "So, what do you think, little guy?"

When a knock sounded at the door, a shiver of goose bumps feathered up and down her arms.

That was odd. It was too late for visitors. She glanced at the clock on the cable box—10:47 p.m.—then looked at Rusty, who was oblivious to the unexpected nocturnal visitor. But what did she expect from a cat?

Too bad she hadn't chosen a dog for a pet when she'd first moved in—a great big Rottweiler named Killer.

The knock sounded again, this time louder and more insistent. Not that she'd planned to ignore it, but deep inside she'd hoped whoever was standing outside would suddenly realize that this was the wrong place.

Isabella went to the door, but she didn't open it. Instead, she lowered her voice in a don't-mess-with-me way. *"Who's there?"*

"It's me, Isabella. J.R."

A wave of relief swept through her, followed by a pang of curiosity. Why was he here? Was he having second thoughts about letting her call the shots?

If so, maybe she ought to be glad that he'd had a change of heart.

Or should she?

Darn those conflicting thoughts and desires, she thought, as she opened the door for him.

As he stepped inside, the small, cozy living room seemed to shrink in his masculine presence. He took off his hat and held it a bit sheepishly. "I'm sorry for barging in on you like this, but I just learned that Cindy Fortune was involved in a suspicious accident this afternoon, and I wasn't comfortable knowing you were home alone."

An eerie shudder of concern settled over her. "What happened?"

"My dad just spoke to the police, and it seems that someone cut her brake line. She crashed through a guardrail and rolled down a slope."

Isabella had never met the woman, but she frowned, saddened by the news. "Who would do such a thing?"

"We don't know. But because of the fires and the notes that people in our families have been getting, everyone is growing more and more uneasy."

She tried to sort through what he was telling her, what those cryptic notes and the fires had really meant. "When I heard about those notes, I assumed they were some kind of prank."

"So did everyone else."

"The fires were a lot more worrisome. But messing with someone's brakes? That's scary, J.R. Is your aunt going to be all right?"

"Yes, but she could have died." He motioned to the sofa. "Why don't we sit down while we talk about this?"

"All right." She sat, and he took a seat beside her.

"My father is on his way out to the Double Crown.

He's going to stay with Lily." J.R. placed his hat on the armrest, then turned to face her. His concern was palpable, and the intensity in his gaze reached somewhere deep inside of her. "I'd like to either stay with you or take you back to my ranch."

She was touched by his offer of protection, yet she wasn't convinced that she really needed it. Was there a threat? Who could possibly want to hurt one of the Fortunes or the Mendozas?

Of course, those threats had taken a dangerous turn, so someone definitely harbored some ill will toward their families.

She turned to J.R., her knee brushing against his. "You don't think it's safe for me to be alone?"

"I'm not sure what any of this means, and I don't know who's behind it or why. So until Cindy comes to and we can learn who might have tampered with her brakes, it's impossible to know who's safe and who isn't." He took her hand, his thumb caressing her skin.

His presence in her home and the intimate gesture were enough to jolt her through and through, and she didn't know what to think—of him, of his news.

She really wasn't frightened by the threat, yet having someone in the house tonight did make her feel a lot better.

"To be honest," he added, "I don't think I could stand it if anything happened to you, Isabella."

The sincerity of his words, of his expression, touched her very soul, and she gave his hand an appreciative squeeze.

"So," he said, "do you want me to sleep on your

sofa? Or do you want to pack some things and come home with me?"

"It doesn't sound as though you're giving me much choice." Yet on the other hand, it didn't seem to matter. If truth be told, she wanted to be with him tonight— threat or no threat.

"I can take you to your father's house, if you'd feel more comfortable there."

She ought to feel more comfortable staying with her dad than with J.R., who was little more than a stranger, but she didn't.

"Do you want to stay here with me?" she asked. "It's a long drive back to your ranch."

"I'm okay with that."

She glanced at the sofa, which she'd purchased because it was smaller than most and wouldn't overwhelm the ten-by-eleven-foot living room. "I'm afraid you might not be very comfortable, though."

There were other options, and they both knew it.

Still, he shrugged. "Don't worry about me. I'll be fine."

She stood, deciding to get a pillow and blanket. Of course, she had a queen-size bed that would be a whole lot more comfortable for him than a sofa his feet would hang over.

"Do you think it would be too difficult for you to sleep in my room with me?"

A boyish grin tugged at his lips. "It shouldn't be a problem. I'm a gentleman."

Did she want him to be one tonight?

A part of her didn't, but she couldn't allow her thoughts to continue in that vein. "We're both adults."

Which meant what—exactly? That they could ignore any adolescent yearnings and do the right thing?

Or that it didn't matter what happened while they shared her bed?

She reached out her hand, and as he took it, she pulled him up to a standing position. "I haven't had a sleepover in a long time. But to be honest, after hearing about your aunt, I'm not sure how well I'd sleep if you left me here alone. I appreciate you driving all the way out here, as well as your offer to stay. I certainly can't insist that you sleep on the sofa and end up with a crick in your neck and back tomorrow."

"If it makes you feel better, I can sleep on top of the covers, and you can sleep under them."

And if she wanted more than that?

Oh, for Pete's sake. What was with her?

He stood before her now, all male, all lean—and willing to sleep wherever she wanted him to.

She placed her hand on his lapel, gripped the fabric of the expensive Western jacket he wore, felt the solid beat of his heart, the warmth and the male essence that bubbled up from deep within him.

For a couple of long, drawn-out seconds, she struggled with her conscience, with whether this man and this moment were right. But her reservations didn't last long.

She met his gaze, and the connection they'd shared for the past few weeks surged with undeniable force.

Could she do it? Could she set aside her list for one night? Could she allow her feminine needs to dictate her actions and just let go?

She wasn't sure, but just considering the possibility warmed her from the inside out.

As if sensing her indecision, he offered her a genuine smile. "As I said, you don't have to be afraid that I'll do anything you don't want me to do. You're still calling all the shots—and that means whether one of us sleeps on top of the blankets or we both slide between the sheets."

"I'm not sure I'm ready for anything between the sheets."

"Then we'll take it one step at a time."

She glanced at the clock, saw that it was merely getting later. "Would you like some coffee? I have decaf. Or are you ready for bed?"

His lips quirked in a sexy smile, and his brow arched sensually.

She crossed her arms, struggling with a smile of her own. "That's *not* what I meant. I was only asking if you were sleepy."

"In that case, then yes. I started the day at four-thirty, so I'm a little tired. But, again, you're in charge."

Something told her that J.R. Fortune didn't cede control to anyone, so the fact that he was yielding to her must mean something.

"All right," she said, accepting the power position and feeling a bit brazen as a result. "Come on. I'll show you to my room."

J.R. followed her into her bedroom, where the queen-size bed with its green-and-purple spread seemed to take up an incredible amount of space. Then she took him to the bathroom. After giving him a fresh towel, she opened the medicine cabinet and pulled out a new tooth-brush before leaving him to get ready for bed.

In the meantime, she filled the litter box and made sure the kitten had fresh water and food. When she was finished, she decided to leave the lamp on in the living room so Rusty wouldn't be left in the dark.

As the water shut off in the shower, she realized the bathroom would soon be free. So she returned to the bedroom and opened the dresser drawer that held her nightgowns. Before she could choose something espe-cially modest, J.R. entered the room, and she quickly snatched the one on top and turned to face him.

He wore only his pants and carried his boots in his hand, his shirt and jacket draped over one arm. She couldn't help noting the broad expanse of his shoulders, the sprinkle of golden brown hair on his bare chest, the set of well-defined abs that indicated he'd been working out regularly—and that he'd been doing so long before he'd ever moved to the ranch.

"I…uh." She nodded toward the bathroom. "I'll change in there. I'll just be a few minutes."

Once she'd ducked into the privacy of the bathroom, she glanced down at the nightgown she held, a slinky, pale yellow number with spaghetti straps. It was one of her newest, but it was also one her sexiest, and she wished she would have put more thought into the choice.

But it was too late now.

Isabella took a quick shower and returned to the bedroom, where she found J.R. stretched out across the top of the bed, still bare-chested and more attractive than ever. She wondered what he usually wore at night.

Boxers? Briefs? Something told her he might even sleep in the raw. For some crazy reason, she wanted to ask.

She didn't, though. Not when she caught him studying her as though he could see right through her satin gown.

Could he?

Maybe she should have opened the drawer and found something else, something flannel and a whole lot less sexy, but she didn't want to make a big deal out of it.

So she pulled back the covers and slid between the sheets, suddenly realizing that she'd forgotten to turn off the light.

"I'll get it," he said.

The lamp she'd left on in the living room for Rusty provided just enough illumination in the room for them to make each other out. She wondered if that was okay with him. If he preferred sleeping in the dark.

He didn't mention anything, so she didn't ask.

As they lay there, a sense of awkwardness settled around her, and she found herself wanting to push past it. So she turned to her side, facing him. "Thank you for throwing that party for me tonight. You really didn't need to do it, but it was lovely, and I'm glad you did. I hadn't really been wanting or expecting anything special."

He turned onto his side as well. "You're special, Isabella. So it's hard not to want to celebrate your birthday."

"Thank you." She studied him for a while, appreciating how handsome he was, how close.

The walls she'd been building around her heart to shut him out began to crumble, and her hand lifted of its own accord. She cupped his cheek, her thumb brushing against his solid, square-cut jaw. Something surged between them, something hot and blood-stirring.

He took her hand and pulled it to his mouth, placing a kiss on her palm. "I can't think of anything I'd like more than to make love to you, but my intentions are completely honorable. So sleep tight, honey."

The term of endearment, the sweetness of his touch, sent her senses reeling, and her heart pounded with anticipation.

If she kissed him now, there would be no decision to make afterward because, as far as self-control went, she'd be toast.

But what if she didn't kiss him? If she didn't chance taking things to a sexual level?

She rose up on an elbow, leaned forward and pressed a good-night kiss on his cheek.

She could have stopped at that—and she probably should have—but some unseen force took over, pressing her to push beyond the gawky, awkward moment she'd been having and to trail her lips along his cheek until they reached his mouth.

Spearmint-laced breaths mingled, and as the kiss slowly deepened, Isabella closed her eyes, caught in a heady arousal of swirling pheromones, musky cologne and the vibrant and steady beat of two hearts pounding out in need.

She ought to pull back, ought to stop, but it felt too good. It also felt right.

That darn list she'd made no longer mattered. Not now. Not when she wanted to feel his arms around her. Not when she wanted to immerse herself in him.

She was lost in a swirl of heat and hunger. Her fingers threaded through his hair, pulling his lips closer, his tongue deeper.

He moaned into her mouth, and she feared she would melt into a simmering pool in the sheets. For a moment, she forgot where they were. Who they were. All she could think about was the raging desire and the promise of something she'd never experienced before.

But as J.R. ran his hand along the curve of her back, caressing the slope of her derriere, she broke the kiss long enough to catch her breath, to search her heart.

"Now what?" she asked.

J.R. couldn't help chuckling. All of a sudden *he* was in charge? "I'll roll over and go to sleep, if you want me to."

Yeah, right. He might roll over, but he'd be damned if he'd be able to sleep with all the testosterone and adrenaline rushing through him.

"It's your call," he added, repeating what he'd told her before. But he'd meant what he said. She was the one who'd been reluctant to get involved. So when they made love, he didn't want her to have any regrets.

She continued to lie there, the struggle playing in the shadows angling over her face.

Damn, he thought. Her uncertainty was becoming more of a turn-on than it should have.

"What if we're sorry about this in the morning?" she asked.

"*I* won't be."

Her smile nearly knocked him off the bed.

Then, ever so slowly, she reached for him. As she

wrapped her arms around his neck and kissed him, his control faded into the heat-charged air. A hot and heavy rush, the likes of which he'd never known, pulsed through him.

The kiss deepened, and J.R. tasted every moist corner of her mouth. All the while, his hands slid along the curve of her back, the slope of her hips.

She began to throw off the blankets, kicking at them and apparently wanting to shed the cloth barriers between them. J.R. was only too happy to oblige.

Before long, they were lying together—man and woman.

She moved closer, arching toward him and driving him wild with need. The desire to make love to her nearly took his breath away.

Threading her fingers in his hair, she gripped him with sexual desperation. A moan formed low in his throat, and he fumbled to remove her pretty gown, hoping he didn't rip the silky material in the process.

It might be a good idea to pull away long enough to undress, but for the life of him, he couldn't stop. He couldn't seem to get enough of the intoxicating kiss; he couldn't get enough of *her.*

As their tongues continued to taste, to seek, to savor, she tugged at the button on his jeans with one hand, while using the other to skim her fingers across his chest. A shiver of arousal shot through his nerve endings, sparking his pulse and sending his blood racing.

He slipped off his pants, then helped her to remove her nightgown, releasing the most perfect breasts he'd ever seen. He ached to touch them, to caress them.

Taking a nipple in his mouth, he tasted, suckled, and she gasped in pleasure. All the while, he continued to stroke, caress, and then to kiss her senseless.

J.R. had never needed so badly to be inside a woman, to lay claim to her body for the rest of his life. And he couldn't wait another minute. He wanted to make love to Isabella now, to glide in and out, filling her completely, bringing her a satisfaction she'd never find with anyone else.

Then she would be his.

When her fingers brushed against his erection, he shuddered. The time was now.

He stopped long enough to reach for his discarded jeans to remove a foil packet from his pocket. Not that he made a point of carrying them around with him in the years after college, but he'd wanted to be prepared for something like this the moment he'd moved to Red Rock and set his sights on Isabella.

She helped him sheathe himself, and as he hovered over her, she opened for him, arching up to meet him, taking all he had and giving all of herself in return.

He thrust deeply, and her body responded to his, melding, molding, until they both reached a peak. She gripped his back, her nails digging into his skin. Never had he experienced a heat like this, a need that went beyond comprehension.

As Isabella cried out in pleasure, he released with her.

Long after the last spasms of pleasure had eased, he continued to hold her tight, afraid to let go.

J.R. didn't know what tomorrow would bring—he'd never imagined that love would feel like this. But one thing was certain. Tonight, he'd made love to the woman he intended to marry.

As the dawn crept through a crack in the curtains, and the scent of their lovemaking lingered in the morning air, J.R. and Isabella lay amid rumpled sheets, his arm lying protectively across her breasts.

He watched her chest softly rise and fall as she slept and savored the faint fragrance of her perfume.

Last night had been out of this world. If he'd ever questioned whether he could settle down with one woman for the rest of his life, he would never wonder about that possibility again. Isabella had been too good to be true.

They hadn't talked about the future yet. And he wasn't entirely sure when they would get around to it— soon, he hoped, because his mind was set.

He wanted Isabella, and that's all there was to it. He just had to convince her that she felt the same way.

But then again, maybe that wouldn't be so hard to do. She certainly hadn't needed much convincing last night.

He brushed away a strand of her hair and placed a kiss on her bare shoulder. Then he slowly drew his other arm out from under her head. Being careful not to wake her, he slipped out of bed.

After a quick shower, he would go into the kitchen and whip up something to eat. Then he would take her breakfast in bed.

What a great way to start the day and to discuss the future.

He would suggest that they start planning a wedding, the sooner the better. And he'd mention that he wanted a minivan full of kids, little boys and girls who would be the perfect blend of their parents and bear the Fortune name.

Hopefully, after all the two of them had shared last night, Isabella was thinking the same thing—that she wanted it all, too. That she wanted it with *him*. That she wanted them to be friends, teammates, lovers.

Once in the bathroom, he scanned the pale green walls, the ivory-colored shower curtain and the matching fluffy towels that hung on the rack.

He reached into the shower stall, turned on the spigots and waited for the water to get warm. He couldn't help noting all the feminine-scented products that lined the shelf behind the commode—a mango-and-pear shampoo with a matching conditioner, an aloe vera splash for after the bath, a variety of lotions.

A slow grin formed. He couldn't wait to smell each one on her, to choose a favorite.

One inside the steamy shower, he spotted a pink razor he hadn't noticed last night. He'd never felt comfortable with women who left their toiletries behind at his house in California. He'd never wanted to give up his space, his privacy. But Isabella wasn't like any woman he'd ever known before.

Boy, how things had changed.

As the water pounded his back, as he lathered the soap and scrubbed his body, he realized that he was looking forward to having Isabella move into his house. And as soon as she did, he'd happily make room for all her things in his bathroom.

Just as he was making room for her in his heart.

Chapter Ten

As the morning sun peered through the window, and the aroma of fresh-perked coffee filled the air, Isabella arched her back and stretched, then slowly opened her eyes.

Only a portion of the sheet was draped over her naked body; the rest was tangled at her feet. For a woman who'd slept alone for almost every night of the past thirty years, her bed felt incredibly empty right now.

She'd slept soundly in the warmth of J.R.'s arms, and she missed not waking with him by her side.

Their night together had been everything she could ever have hoped for and more. He was an incredible lover—the best.

Yet she still hadn't been able to kick the reservations she had about them having a future together.

Now what? she asked herself. Where would they go from here? Where *should* they go?

She wished the answer was simple, but it wasn't.

To be honest, she truly *wanted* to love J.R., and she wanted him to be the special man in her life. But she just wasn't sure.

There was so much more to life and to love than great sex, although she would have been hard-pressed to argue that point last night. And even as good as their lovemaking had been, she still felt torn about where to go from here.

A part of her wanted more time to think, yet another part wanted to call J.R. back to bed.

She didn't do either.

Her first thought was that the problem was him, that he fell short of what she needed in a mate. Yet as she considered the man she'd gotten to know over the past few weeks and what they'd shared last night, she had to face another possibility, whether she wanted to or not.

The problem just might be her.

She rolled to the side, taking the sheet with her. But her being the problem wasn't something she wanted to ponder right now. She didn't particularly like thinking of herself as a commitment-phobe.

Surely, it wasn't that.

Maybe she was just carrying some excess baggage.

Her parents had shared a passionate relationship before hitting the skids and splitting up. They'd both gone on to other relationships that had appeared lasting.

Her dad had married again and had several kids before losing his wife to cancer. And he'd said they'd been happy.

But while her stepfather had loved her mother, Isabella didn't think they'd been as happy as they should have been.

So was that the problem? Was that holding her back?

The smell of coffee grew stronger, and she found herself craving a cup.

J.R. must be in the kitchen. Should she drag herself out of bed and be a better hostess?

"Good morning." He entered the bedroom with a cup in his hand. "I brought you some coffee."

She offered him a smile, but didn't trust herself to speak. Instead, she studied the handsome man who was only wearing a pair of sky-blue boxers, his hair still damp and mussed from the shower.

Could a man be any sexier than that?

Isabella ought to be craving a lot more than caffeine, and while she was, actually, the sense of awkwardness returned full force.

J.R. took a seat on the edge of the mattress. "I'm not as good in the kitchen as Evie, but I managed to whip up some scrambled eggs and toast for you."

"You didn't need to do that."

"I wanted to."

His efforts were sweet, and while she was touched by his thoughtfulness, he seemed…out of place—and not just in the kitchen or her studio apartment, but in her life.

Still, she managed a smile and tried to shake off the lingering negativity.

What was with her? There had to be a hundred women in the county who'd jump at the chance to wake up in J.R. Fortune's arms.

He set the coffee mug on the nightstand, then picked up a silver-framed photograph of her parents—one of the few she had of them together.

"I recognize Luis," he said. "Is this your mom?"

She nodded. "A friend of theirs took that shot. My dad found it in an old box he had in storage and gave it to me. He knew I'd like having it."

"They look young. But happy."

"I think they were—for a while." Until their differences chilled the passion that had once burned between them. "But the marriage didn't last."

"Young couples face a lot more obstacles than older ones," J.R. said. "Men and women in their thirties and forties usually have a solid sense of direction, as well as a greater ability to weather storms and make things work."

Was he hinting that she shouldn't worry about the two of them facing the same trials and troubles if they chose to walk down the aisle?

She couldn't quite buy it. Isabella's mother had been a little older when she married for the second time, but in order to "weather the storms and make things work," she'd had to give up so much of herself—her family, the people she knew in San Antonio, her heritage.

"Hey, look who's here." J.R. stooped, picked up Rusty and, after cuddling him for a moment, placed him on the bed with Isabella.

She sat up, pulling the sheet up to cover her breasts, and took the kitten in her arms. "Hi, little guy. How was your first night in your new home, huh?"

The kitten purred softly.

Isabella glanced at J.R., who seemed to be studying her intently. "Thanks for getting him for me. I think it's going to be nice having a pet."

"Looks like he's going to be the lucky one."

She grinned, then stroked the kitten again.

"You're obviously an animal lover. Do you like kids, too?"

Uh-oh. Was he hinting at them creating a family? Or was that merely her imagination?

"They're okay," she said, downplaying her hopes for a family of her own.

In truth, she'd love to have children—if it was with the right guy.

But was J.R. that guy?

He seemed so sure of himself, so sure of *them*. She truly wished she could share his confidence.

She had feelings for him—strong ones—but she couldn't quite bring herself to call it love.

Their lovemaking, of course, was out of this world. But could they make a commitment to each other that would bind their hearts and lives forever?

She honestly couldn't say.

What if J.R. got tired of playing cowboy and wanted to go back to California and the successful life he had there?

Isabella wouldn't be happy living anywhere other than San Antonio or Red Rock. And divorce wasn't going to be an option for her, especially if they had children. There was no way she'd do to her kids what her mother had done to her. So what options were left?

"What are your plans for today?" J.R. asked.

"I have some work to do," she said. "So I'm going to the studio."

"Why don't you pack some things and come to the ranch? I can pick you up or send a driver for you."

She'd been a little uneasy at night, but in the light of day, she felt much better. "I'll be okay."

"I'm sure you're probably right." He placed his hand on her hip. "But that doesn't mean I'll feel comfortable until whoever is threatening our families is apprehended."

Okay, so there *was* a real threat out there. But J.R.'s protective streak was just a tad unsettling. Was it a sign that he was controlling, as her stepfather had been?

She couldn't dismiss the possibility.

"Thanks, J.R. I appreciate your concern." She slowly pulled off the sheets, climbed out of bed and put Rusty on the floor. "I'll be careful—*and* I'll keep my eyes open."

Then she headed for the privacy of the bathroom and closed the door, pushing the button that secured the lock.

She certainly hadn't had any reservations about getting romantically involved with him last night.

But now, in the light of day, reality had set in.

Late that afternoon, as Isabella worked on the loom in her studio, the small cowbell on the door chimed, alerting her to someone's arrival.

"I'll be right there," she called, as she slowed the loom to a stop.

It was too bad that Sarah wasn't here to deal with the customers, but she'd asked for some time off to go shopping. Toby was taking her out to dinner this evening, and she'd wanted to find a new outfit to wear.

The girl still had stars in her eyes, and Isabella was happy for her. The two certainly seemed like a good match—in spite of their age.

As Isabella made her way to the front of the studio, she spotted Julie Osterman studying the display near the window. Julie, who worked for the Fortune Foundation, was a teacher and counselor of troubled teens.

"Hello," Isabella said, as she approached.

Julie turned and smiled. "I hope I'm not bothering you."

"Not at all."

The thirtysomething woman with light brown hair and blue eyes was attractive, Isabella decided, but she'd be even prettier if she chose brighter colors and more stylish clothes.

Today she was dressed for comfort in a black top, flowing pants and a pair of clogs. Her jewelry, though, was not only unusual but interesting.

"I really like your necklace," Isabella said. "And those bracelets, too."

"Thanks." Julie lifted her arm, glanced at the bangles. "I found them at an estate sale and thought they were unique."

Isabella wondered why she'd stopped by. "Is there anything I can help you with?"

"As a matter of fact, there is. The Spring Fling is coming up, and Susan Fortune Eldridge and I are in charge of the vendors. We wondered if you'd like to exhibit your blankets and tapestries."

Each May, the Fortune Foundation sponsored the Spring Fling, the proceeds of which funded many of their charity projects. Everyone in Red Rock looked forward to the event, which not only included a dance, but also a carnival and various art exhibits.

"Can we count on you to take part?" Julie asked.

"Of course." Isabella was always happy to be included in a worthy cause. "And I'll donate a portion of my sales to the foundation."

"We certainly appreciate your generosity," Julie said, as she turned back to the tapestry she'd been perusing. "Your work is beautiful. I can understand why Susan would insist that we talk to you."

"Thank you."

Julie looked at several more pieces, then said, "I've got several other stops to make, so I'd better go. Thanks to participating in the Spring Fling—I'll see you there."

Isabella watched the woman leave. She'd just started back to the loom when the telephone rang.

It could be anyone, she supposed. But she had a feeling it was J.R. calling again.

If so, she still didn't know what to tell him. She was torn between wanting to see him again and maintaining her distance.

How would she be able to backpedal on their relationship if they kept getting ever more deeply involved?

J.R. sat in his office, the telephone receiver in his hand as he waited for Isabella to answer. The fact that she still hadn't committed to driving out to the ranch this evening had him a bit perplexed.

He'd been so sure that everything was falling into place that her sudden indecision made him feel off balance. Okay, so she hadn't actually made any real decisions one way or the other. But how could she not want a relationship with him after last night? Didn't their chemistry prove anything?

It made no sense.

The phone rang several times before she said, "Hello, this is Isabella."

"How's it going?" he asked.

She paused for a beat. "All right. How about you?"

He didn't know yet. Not until she gave him the answer he was looking for. He did opt to tell her what he had in store for them this evening. "I've got a quiet dinner for two planned."

"I'm still not sure if I can make it," she said.

The last time they'd talked, she'd told him she had work to do, so he didn't want to push too hard. "You don't have to give me an answer now. Call me later."

"All right."

As J.R. hung up the telephone, he stood with the receiver in his hand for the longest time. Something was wrong. Isabella was pulling away from him, and he couldn't figure out why.

He'd called her twice today, and both times she'd claimed to be busy. He suspected that was true, but he was having a hard time buying it.

"Is something wrong?" Evie asked from the doorway.

He glanced up and managed a smile. "No, everything's fine."

"I've got the table set, and dinner is in the oven. All you need to do is serve it and enjoy."

"Thanks, Evie. When are you leaving?"

"At five. Is that still all right with you?"

"Absolutely. Enjoy the night off."

"I intend to." She glanced around the office floor. "Where's Baron?"

"Snoozing at my feet."

She smiled. "After that close call he had, I want to make sure he doesn't sneak outside without someone looking after him."

They'd nearly lost the dog, which would have been tough. Yet not as tough as losing Isabella.

As the sound of Evie's footsteps disappeared down the hall, J.R. pondered his dilemma. How much effort was he prepared to put into a relationship that still hadn't left the ground? If the woman was anyone other than Isabella, he'd have to say not much. But as it was...

A male voice interrupted his thoughts. "Excuse me, boss."

J.R. looked up to see Frank in the doorway, his hat in his hand. "What's up?"

"We've got a problem with the well in the south pasture. We might need a new pump."

"Why don't you call it a day, Frank. I know you have plans for tonight. I'll deal with the irrigation problem."

Trouble was, the only pressing problem that J.R. wanted to deal with right now was Isabella.

What was holding her back?

And would it be too much for him to overcome?

Two days after the accident, the Red Rock police still had no idea who'd tried to kill Cindy Fortune. But she had her own suspicions.

"Since you have plenty of family in the area," the

nurse said, as she waited for Cindy to sign the discharge papers, "I assume you have a place to stay and someone to look after you while you recover."

Cindy would never ask to stay with family members. And even if one of her kids invited her to, she would decline. She valued her privacy too much.

"I'm going to a hotel," she responded.

"Is someone coming to pick you up?" the nosy nurse asked, as she handed Cindy the papers to sign.

What did it matter?

Cindy picked up the pen, taking care not to exert too much pressure on her sprained finger. After scratching out her name, she pushed the paperwork back to the woman. "I'm not about to bother anyone, so I'm going to take a cab. Will you call one for me?"

"I'll see what I can do."

Ten minutes later, Cindy was seated in the backseat of a taxi and headed for the nearest hotel. But in spite of a headache that continued to come and go, she wasn't eager to check into a room and lie down.

Instead, she would confront the only person who might think he was smart enough to get away with making a murder look like an accident.

As the cab drove through Red Rock, she noticed a black Corvette parked in front of the Blue Bonnet Café, just as pretty as you please.

Well, now. Would you look at that? This must be her lucky day. That had to be Lloyd Fredericks's car.

"Stop!" she ordered the cabbie. "Turn around. I want you to go back to that café. But don't leave. Wait for me."

"I'll need to keep the meter running," he said.

"I realize that." She reached into her purse and pulled out a ten. "I'll give you the rest and a nice tip when I come out. I won't be long."

As Cindy climbed out of the cab, she winced in pain. Damn. Everything hurt like a son of a gun.

She shut the passenger door, then strode into the café. Once inside, she searched each booth and table until she spotted Lloyd seated near the back, reading a newspaper and drinking a mug of coffee.

The handsome man was alone, which would make a confrontation easy.

For the past two days, Cindy had thought long and hard about who could have possibly tampered with her brakes, who might have wanted to see her dead. And, quite frankly, only one person came to mind, and that person was her son-in-law.

He'd never liked her. Never respected the fact that she'd done her best to be a good mother, no matter what some of her ungrateful children might say about that.

And who was he to complain?

No one else might give a turkey's rump about what the man did each day after leaving home. But Cindy knew. Not much got by her.

As she made her way to her son-in-law's table, she studied him carefully. He was fast approaching his fortieth birthday, if he hadn't passed it already. With those soulful eyes, he was still good-looking, Cindy realized. But she'd known the type. He'd been a spoiled, sullen kid who'd evolved into a smooth-talking charmer.

But worse than that, Lloyd Fredericks wasn't a man to be trusted.

Challenging him might undo some of the positive steps she'd made with Frannie the other day. But she couldn't let him get away with what he'd done.

No one messed with Cindy Fortune.

"Well, if it isn't Lloyd Fredericks," Cindy said. "As I live and breathe. I'm in luck."

Lloyd didn't immediately look up from his paper. He clearly recognized her voice, as well as the sarcastic undertone.

"Oh, wait," she said, finally gaining his attention. "I suppose my lucky day was when I survived that little…*accident*."

Lloyd looked up from his reading long enough to snarl and ask, "Who peed in your stewed prunes?"

She wanted to pinch his little head off. Instead, she crossed her arms, stopping as soon as she remembered how sore her chest was, thanks to the monstrous bruise she'd received from the seat belt and the airbag that had saved her life. As soon as she swallowed her pain, she cleared her throat and narrowed her eyes. "Someone tampered with my brakes, Lloyd. And I have every reason to believe it was you."

He turned to face her, a scowl marring his normally handsome face. "Are you losing it? You're about that age, aren't you?"

She stiffened, ready to claw his eyes out.

He must have sensed her ire, because he softened just a tad and asked, "Why would I do something stupid like that? What would I have to gain? It's not as though you have any insurance policies and made Frannie or me the beneficiary."

"How would you know?" she asked.

He laughed, one of those deep, don't-underestimate-me laughs. "Maybe I checked."

Maybe he had.

"Listen here," Lloyd said. "I'm not saying that anyone would be terribly disappointed to hear about your death, but don't look at me. I didn't do it."

"I *am* looking at you." Cindy wasn't at all sure that she believed him. He'd always been selfish. Would he stoop to murder?

She hadn't thought so, but who knew what motivated a man like Lloyd Fredericks? And just how far did his greed go?

"I'm just about to get everything I've worked for," he added. "So someone else must have it in for you."

She suspected it went much further than that.

Lloyd and his father owned an investment company called Fredericks Financial, which Cindy had learned wasn't all that solvent. As she said, it paid to do a little research and to know these things.

He shrugged. "I'd be a fool to tamper with your brakes. You'll have to keep digging for someone to blame for your near-death experience."

He took a sip of coffee, then picked up his newspaper, shutting her out.

But not for good.

Chapter Eleven

That evening, Isabella stood in front of her closet, trying to find something to wear. J.R. had invited her to have dinner with him in the renovated courtyard of his house, but she couldn't seem to work up the proper enthusiasm for this get-together.

All day she'd thought about calling him and telling him that something unexpected had come up, that she couldn't find time to drive out to the ranch and spend the evening with him after all.

But she hadn't. Deep inside, she desperately wanted to see him, to be with him.

She truly cared about J.R. And she wanted to cling to his kindness, to his strength. Whether she liked it or not, he had claimed a piece of her heart. She just wasn't sure how much.

And that was the problem. J.R. wanted more than a one-on-one commitment. He wanted marriage and babies and the whole nine yards, which frightened her way more than it should. After all, she'd been the first of her friends to make that single-no-more pact. So she ought to be thrilled.

Sure, she felt a definite buzz of excitement whenever she thought about him, but she couldn't fully let go of her apprehension.

She left the closet door open and sat on the edge of bed, where she and J.R. had made love just hours before. She'd washed the sheets this afternoon and put the spread back in place, but even though the room appeared to be in order, it would never be the same again.

And neither would she—no matter what she chose to do tonight.

Still, the questions remained. What did she feel for J.R.? And what did she want from a relationship with him?

Would she be content with an affair?

The answer to that one was easy. It would have to be all or nothing for her. But she feared that "having it all" with J.R. simply wasn't possible.

Isabella exhaled a weary sigh. As often as she'd tossed her dilemma around today, she still had no answer. But she couldn't put it off any longer. She was going to drive out to the ranch after all.

Maybe seeing J.R. again, talking to him, would make things crystal clear in her mind. And if not? She'd come home right after dinner.

So she stood, returned to the open closet and pulled out the new black dress she'd purchased on a recent shopping trip with Jane.

Isabella usually steered clear of dull, mournful colors, but she'd liked the cut of this particular dress, as well as the fit. So she'd bought it, planning to wear fancy jewelry to give it more pizzazz.

But she didn't feel especially decadent right now and decided to leave her jewelry at home.

Besides, the color and somber style seemed appropriate tonight. So she removed it from the hanger and put it on.

Next she applied her makeup, combed out her long tresses and slipped into a pair of heels.

All the while, the battle between her heart and her mind waged on.

Even with the time J.R. had given her to think about the direction she wanted to go, the knot in her tummy continued to twist and turn. And she feared it would do so until she finally decided to run for the hills or to dig in her heels and give a relationship with J.R. a chance.

"I'll let you know about dinner later," she'd told him earlier. So before she headed to the ranch, she picked up the phone to tell him she was on her way.

Evie, her voice more lighthearted than usual, answered.

Had J.R.'s housekeeper/cook been expecting Isabella to call? Or was something going on at the ranch tonight, something J.R. hadn't mentioned?

The man was full of surprises, and she wondered if he'd been plotting something else to charm her, to force her hand.

"It's Isabella," she said. "Is J.R. available?"

"No, he went out to the south pasture and hasn't come in yet."

Isabella wondered if something had come up on his part and hoped that it had. On a scale of one to ten, she was only around a five when it came to the strength of her decision to go to the ranch and let things fall where they may.

"He invited me to dinner," Isabella said, "but if he's busy—"

"Oh, no," Evie said. "He's not too busy. Dinner's in the oven. And the table is already set. He's looking forward to having you here tonight."

Isabella didn't doubt that. And now he had Evie on board and determined to make things work.

"There's a chance I'll be gone before he comes in from the pasture," Evie added. "When we discussed the menu, I told him I'd leave the meal in the oven. But I forgot to mention that I put the salad in the fridge. So will you please let him know that?"

"Where are you going?" Isabella asked. Not that it was any of her business, but Evie lived with J.R. at the ranch. And it would be dark soon. Had J.R. sent Evie off for the night so he and Isabella would be alone in the house?

"Believe it or not," Evie said, "I'm going on a date."

The enthusiasm in her voice was hard to ignore, which indicated that J.R. hadn't had a hand in that.

"How exciting," Isabella said. "Who are you going out with? Anyone I know?"

"Yes. Frank Damon, the foreman."

Isabella couldn't say she was at all surprised. She'd seen the way the man had looked at Evie.

"It's just dinner and a movie," Evie added.

"That sounds like fun."

"Yes, it does. I just hope asking me out was all Frank's idea. J.R. is so good at orchestrating things, and I know that he's really looking forward to being alone with you tonight."

"I'm sure Frank is looking forward to the date, too," she said. Yet she, too, couldn't help wondering if J.R. had been involved. He *was* a master at orchestrating.

"J.R. certainly planned a nice party for me," Isabella said. "And he had very little time to pull it together."

Evie chuckled. "I know. He insisted on everything being perfect for the party, from the guest list to the menu to the music. I have to tell you, when J.R. Fortune sets his mind to doing something, he makes it happen."

And he'd clearly set his mind on having Isabella.

Maybe that's what had been bothering her all along.

A sense of uneasiness settled over her as she thought about the lengths her stepfather had gone to get her mother out of Texas, to keep Isabella from her father.

To make them both forget who they really were.

Last night, J.R. had told Isabella that she was in charge. That she was calling the shots.

But was she?

Had their lovemaking only been part of a carefully planned seduction? One that had convinced her that going to bed with him had been her idea?

A sour taste formed in Isabella's mouth, and she cleared her throat. "Since J.R. can't come to the phone, will you please give him a message?"

"Sure."

"Tell him I'm really sorry, but I won't be able to see him tonight."

"Oh, no," Evie said. "He's going to be terribly disappointed."

Not any more than Isabella would have been if she'd shown up for another carefully orchestrated seduction.

J.R. entered the house and went directly to the courtyard. He wanted to make sure that Evie had followed his instructions to the letter.

As he'd requested, the lights in the alcove were dimmed, and candles sat on the linen-draped table, ready to be lit. Water gurgled in the fountain, and lush green plants and flowers hung from hooks on the walls. All he had to do was hand-pick the music on the stereo, and the setting of tonight's dinner would be perfect.

Before heading for the bathroom to shower, he went to his bedroom to check and make sure everything was just the way he wanted it. And it was.

On the nightstand, near the bed, sat a small black velvet box. He lifted the lid and peered inside, saw the diamond sparkle. It had belonged to his mother. After the day he'd kissed Isabella in the field of wildflowers, he'd known that she was the one who would wear it. So he'd taken it to the jeweler and had it cleaned.

Was it too much?

Was it too soon?

Having second thoughts, he placed it in the drawer, where it would be ready when he decided the time was right.

After taking a shower, he went to the kitchen to check on dinner. He found Evie pulling something from the oven, something that smelled delicious.

"I see everything is ready," he said.

When she turned to face him, he saw that her hair was curled and combed, that she wore lipstick and mascara.

"You look great," he said.

Evie offered him a flustered grin and fingered the side of her hair. "Thanks, J.R. It's been so long since I fixed myself up for a man that I nearly forgot how."

"It must be like riding a bike," he said, "because it certainly came back to you. You're going to knock Frank's socks off."

A happy smile burst across her face. "I sure hope so. But you can't believe how nervous I am. You'd think I'd never gone out on a date before."

"You'll only be nervous for a minute or two. And if it helps, I can assure you that Frank's fretting a bit, too."

She sobered. "Do you think he regrets asking me?"

J.R. chuckled. "Not in the least. It's been a long time for him, too."

"What a pair we're going to be tonight."

Actually, J.R. thought, the two might make a nice pair long after the first date was over.

"By the way," he said, "did you happen to hear from Isabella?"

He hated the idea of calling her again. He wasn't normally the pushy type.

Evie's smile faded. "Yes, I'm afraid so. She isn't going to be able to come tonight."

Disappointment slammed into J.R., but he tried not to let it show. "Did she say why?"

"Just that something came up."

J.R. had never dealt with losing, had never really had

to. But he had to face the truth. He was losing Isabella, and there wasn't much he could do about it.

Hell, he wasn't even sure he should try.

Isabella glanced in the mirror and realized that she was all dressed up with no place to go. Not that she wanted to *go* anywhere.

Maybe she ought to take a long, hot bubble bath. Afterward, she could put on a pair of comfortable sweats and pour herself a glass of wine, then kick back and watch television.

She went to the cupboard, thinking she'd open a bottle of merlot and pour herself a glass. But apparently, she'd opened the last one when she'd hosted a girls' night last fall.

There was a wine shop not too far from here. She could drive there and pick up another, but since she really only wanted a single serving, she'd probably end up tossing the rest down the sink.

She could, she suppose, forgo it completely, but tonight she would really welcome the light buzz a single glass would provide.

"What do you think?" she asked the kitten, who was batting around a little felt mouse. "Should I just stay home and forget it?"

Rusty didn't seem to care one way or the other.

Of course, if she hung out here, she might have to deal with J.R. if he decided to call. Or what if he drove out to talk to her in person? She wouldn't put it past a determined man like him.

Truthfully? She was avoiding him for a reason, and

while she'd eventually have to tell him that she didn't want to see him again, it didn't have to be today.

In the past, whenever she'd needed someone to talk to, she'd always called Jane. But now that Jane was practically living with Jorge, Isabella couldn't possibly pop in on her. So her options were fading fast.

The portable phone rested on the counter, and as she picked it up, she noted a flyer advertising the Trail's End, a new nightclub down the street. She'd set the ad aside to remind herself that she might want to get a few single friends together and check it out sometime.

Since the Trail's End was within walking distance, there was no need to drive.

Feeling somewhat rebellious, she uttered, "Oh, why not? It just might get my mind off J.R."

So she locked up the apartment and walked three blocks to Trail's End, a place that seemed to be hopping with the happy hour set.

As she entered, she noted the music blaring in the background as a laid-back crowd talked and laughed among themselves. Intent upon having that glass of wine and then leaving, she shook off the all-by-herself uneasiness and took a seat at a small table.

Too bad she couldn't just order a glass of wine to go. That way, she could head home, fill up the tub and relax. But she knew better than to ask. They'd never allow her to leave the building.

A shapely blond waitress wearing Daisy Duke shorts and a crop top laid a cocktail napkin on the table. "Hi, there. Can I get you something to drink?"

"Do you have a wine list?"

The woman, who had a name tag that said Sally, handed her a small, sandwich board-type sign from another table and smiled. "If you're a connoisseur, you won't be impressed."

"I'm really just a lightweight, but a glass of wine sounded good tonight." Maybe it would help her sleep.

"I tried to tell the owner that we ought to offer a better selection," Sally said, "but he'd rather offer an extensive beer list."

Isabella glanced at her options. "I'll have the merlot."

"You got it." The woman stopped at another table before heading back to the bar.

"Excuse me," said a man in his late thirties to early forties. "Are you Isabella Mendoza?"

"Yes, why?"

"I thought I recognized you." He grinned, his eyes glimmering. "A man wouldn't forget a pretty gal with hair like yours."

"Have we met?" she asked.

"No, not exactly. But I've seen you from a distance. You hang out a lot in Red Rock—at Red. You're a niece of José and Maria."

"Yes, I am." She scanned his face, trying to remember if she'd ever seen him, but she didn't think she had. He was an attractive man and would have made an impression on her.

"Is that seat taken?" he asked.

Was he hitting on her? It was hard to say. Apparently, he knew her family, so she didn't think it would hurt to share her table with him. Besides, she wouldn't be here that long. "Go ahead and sit down."

He flashed her a charming smile and took the seat across from her. "I've only been in here a time or two, but it's an exciting place. Do you come here often?"

"This is my first time."

He nodded as though making a mental note of it. "Are you meeting someone?"

Should she lie? Tell him that she was waiting for a friend? She was usually pretty careful about what she told strangers, but he seemed like a nice guy. And he knew her family. She was probably being overcautious.

"I'm supposed to meet a friend for dinner," she said, opting to be vague and to at least touch on the truth.

They chatted for a bit, sticking to the basics—the atmosphere at the Trail's End, the service.

"The band is pretty good," he said. "Don't you think?"

She hadn't really been listening, but she supposed it was okay.

The cocktail waitress returned with Isabella's wine, then took the man's order—a gin and tonic.

"Put her wine on my tab." He reached for his credit card and handed it to the waitress. "Thanks, Sally."

Again, he seemed nice enough, she supposed. "I didn't catch your name."

"It's Lloyd."

The name didn't trigger her memory at all, so she was pretty sure she hadn't met him before.

Strange...

His cell phone rang, and he pulled it from the holder on his belt. He glanced down at the lighted display, furrowed his brow, then looked back at her. "I'm sorry, you're going to have to excuse me. I'd let it ring through, but this might be important."

"Of course."

He flipped open the cell and answered without saying hello. "This is a bad time, Josh."

His brow furrowed again, this time deeper. "What? Yes, I cut off your card."

Isabella could only glean one side of the conversation, and she had to strain to hear the man's voice over the din in the bar.

He leaned back in what appeared to be enjoyment. "Because I didn't want you spending your money on that little—" He listened for a moment. "Stop it right there."

His smile faded completely as he straightened. Even in the dim bar she could see him tense in anger. "No, you listen to me, Josh. It's over. You're going to stop seeing—"

His eye twitched, and he frowned, as though the caller may have ended the call before he had a chance to finish. For a moment, he looked absolutely livid. Unbalanced. Then he snapped the phone shut.

He turned to her and forced a smile. "Telemarketers drive me crazy."

That was no telemarketer, Isabella realized. It was someone named Josh. But she didn't want to talk about it anymore than he probably did.

"It sounds like you need to go," she said.

"Not right now. It'll wait."

Sally returned with Lloyd's drink. When she left, he looked across the table at Isabella. "I heard you were doing some work out at J.R. Fortune's ranch."

The fact that he seemed to know so much about her, when she didn't know squat about him, didn't sit right. "Have you met J.R.?"

"Yep. I'm in pretty tight with the Fortunes." He took a sip of his drink. "It's too bad about all the trouble they've been having."

"The trouble?"

"You know. The fire at the Double Crown, Cindy's car accident."

Isabella wasn't comfortable discussing J.R. or his family in public, so she changed the subject.

They made some small talk for a while, and when his drink was empty and hers merely half gone, he motioned to Sally and asked for another round.

Isabella realized that he hadn't actually hit on her— yet, but it sure felt as though he might. And while she wasn't interested, she didn't mind having a momentary diversion.

Maybe the night would turn out better than she'd thought.

After taking a second drink order from the guy at table twelve, Sally returned to the bar.

"Looks like our friend Lloyd is about to score again," Todd, the bartender said.

"I'm sure he's working on it." She blew out a sigh. "I can't stand Lloyd Fredericks. He drives up in that fancy black sports car of his, then parks in back so no one sees it and knows he's here. He's such a jerk. He's always hitting on women and pretending to be single."

"You'd think a woman would be able to see through that," Todd said.

"Yeah, well the one he's with tonight seems nice enough. I hate seeing women fall for guys like that."

"Maybe you should warn her."

"I just might." Sally chuffed. "And I ought to have a little talk with his wife. I'll bet she doesn't know her husband has been here almost every night this week."

"You don't normally get involved," he said.

"I know. Don't worry. I won't call her. She probably already knows."

Todd slowly shook his head. "His wife is related to the Fortunes, isn't she?"

"I think so. At least, that's what I heard. I think her name is Francie or Frannie. Something like that."

"Nice family. Too bad they got stuck with a loser like Lloyd."

"By the way," Sally said, "I'm going to need another merlot plus a gin and tonic."

"You'll have to wait," he said. "I've got a bunch of teetotalers at table seven and I've got six virgin strawberry daiquiris to make."

"I'll wait," she said. "Or better yet, I think I'll take a potty break. I've been holding it for an hour."

"You got it."

Sally headed for the restroom. Once inside, she stopped at the mirror long enough to see that she needed to reapply her lipstick, then she stepped into the nearest stall.

When she came out, she noticed the attractive brunette entering, the woman who'd been sitting with

Lloyd Fredericks. With that gorgeous black dress and the long, flowing hair, she was even prettier in the light.

When the woman smiled, Sally returned it, then bit down on her bottom lip.

Their eyes met a second time, and Sally couldn't hold her tongue any longer. "Excuse me. I make it a point not to butt into things that aren't my business, but you seem like a nice woman. And I figure you probably just met that guy."

The brunette arched a delicate brow. "What are you getting at?"

"Just that you need to watch out for him. He's not only married, but he cheats—*a lot.*"

The brunette was visibly shaken by the news. "Are you kidding?"

"Nope. I'm sorry to be the bearer of bad news. But I'd feel worse if you took him home and I didn't warn you."

"I wasn't going to take him home. But thanks for the heads-up."

Sally nodded, then turned on the faucet and washed her hands. When she finished and activated the automatic dryer on the wall, she glanced around the bathroom.

The brunette was already gone.

While waiting for Isabella to return to his table, Lloyd downed another drink. Damn, but she was beautiful. And a lot more sophisticated than the gals he usually pursued. But he was up for something new tonight. Something exciting.

He flagged Sally, who took her time responding.

The snob. He'd asked her out a time or two, but she was made of ice.

When she finally made her way to the table, she asked, "What can I get you?"

"Another gin and tonic," he said.

As Sally turned her back, Lloyd's cell phone rang.

He glanced at the lighted display, but didn't immediately recognize the number. He thought about letting it go to voice mail, but answered anyway. "Hello?"

His brow furrowed as soon as he heard the familiar voice.

"Why are you calling *me?*" he asked.

"Because I know what you're up to, and it's not going to work."

Lloyd stiffened. "You listen here. I don't know what you've imagined or what you've got up your sleeve, but I don't like threats."

"Not only do I know your big secret, Lloyd, but I'm going to tell the world unless you give me what I want."

Lloyd's blood pressure shot through the roof. No way was he going to lose everything he'd worked for, not when it was within his reach.

And he damn sure wasn't going to let anyone blackmail him, especially tonight. So he ended the call without further comment.

He did, however, have half a notion to leave right now and put a stop to all that crap. But it could wait until tomorrow.

He glanced around the bar.

What the hell was taking Isabella so long?

He glanced around the room. the woman, it seemed had vanished without saying goodbye.

Chapter Twelve

Isabella walked home from the Trail's End at a pretty good clip. By the time she turned down her street, the high heels were causing her feet to ache, but she was so angry and frustrated, she didn't care.

She wouldn't have given Lloyd What's-his-name more than a passing glance, so it's not as though his deceitful charm had hurt her. But somehow, she felt violated on behalf of every woman in the world—married or single.

It sickened her to think that he was hanging out in nightclubs, preying on the lonely. And all the while, Mrs. What's-her-name waited at home, unsuspecting.

Her thoughts drifted to J.R., who waited at the ranch for her. Dinner was in the oven, Evie had said.

A pang of guilt poked at Isabella's chest. She hadn't exactly done the right thing herself today, either. She'd bailed out on J.R.'s invitation, and she hadn't even had the courtesy to tell him herself. Instead, she'd asked Evie to relay the message.

Once back at her apartment, Isabella kicked off her shoes and turned on the radio, trying to do something to still the silence that mocked the compulsion to cry her heart out. But the music didn't help, and she feared that she only had herself to blame.

What had provoked her to chat with a stranger anyway?

Right this moment, she had a decent man who deserved a little heart-to-heart chat with her. Yet she'd chosen to avoid him rather than make a decision or admit what was holding her back.

She'd wanted to blame her hesitancy on the fact that there might be something lacking in him. But now it seemed as though she was the one who'd fallen short.

What was so hard about telling him that she didn't want to cede control to anyone? That she was proud of her heritage and wanted a man who could respect that?

Why couldn't she just admit that she was wildly attracted to him, that she might even love him? That it scared the hell out of her to think of giving in?

She slipped off her clothes and pulled a pair of gray sweats out of the closet. She couldn't wait to get into something loose and comfortable.

She placed her dress on the stack of clothing she was planning to take to the dry cleaners. It wasn't as though it was soiled or couldn't be worn again—she'd only had it on briefly. But she wanted to shuck all reminders of the jerk she'd just met.

If she ever got seriously involved with anyone, he'd

be honorable and trustworthy. A man who would respect his wedding vows and go the distance to make their marriage work.

A man like J.R.? an inner voice asked.

The question hung in the air, and her movements stilled.

To be honest? J.R. certainly hadn't given her any reason to believe he was anything but that kind of man.

His attributes, many of which she'd once downplayed, began to flicker on a screen in her mind, one after the other.

His dancing eyes.

That one-dimpled grin.

Those broad shoulders and taut abs.

His lovemaking skills.

But it wasn't just his physical attributes and talents coming to mind, it was his actions, too.

He went out in the fields and worked along with his men each day, getting dirty and sometimes coming home late to dinner.

And what about that birthday party he'd planned for her? It had gone off without a hitch, thanks to his careful planning.

Then there was the beautiful jewelry he'd chosen because it had reminded him of her.

He'd also chased down those kids at Fiesta and gotten Rusty for her, just because he'd sensed that she'd been enamored of the tiny ball of fur. He'd given her a chance to try out having a pet and had even been willing to step in and provide a home for the kitten if she felt she couldn't handle the added responsibility of pet ownership.

Oh, for Pete's sake. She'd also been reluctant to

assume the responsibility of a romantic relationship, without any guarantees that it might last. But wasn't that what it was all about? Loving someone enough to run that risk? To step out in faith and to make it work?

She ran her fingers through her hair and sat on the edge of the bed. She just realized that she had more baggage than she'd thought. What kind of woman would take all that J.R. had offered and throw it back in his face?

Okay, so he hadn't exactly offered her the moon, but she'd clearly known that he was headed in that direction.

What kind of woman *was* she?

Who was she?

She stood and walked to the mirror, where she looked at the image that stared back at her—the waifish eyes, the drab clothes. She might have missed it before, but right now, she could see every little hurt, every little scar that she'd ever had as a child.

Deep inside, she suspected that there might be a little girl, lost and lonely, trying to stand out in the crowd. Trying to pin her heart on someone who wouldn't let her down.

So what made her think that J.R. would let her down?

Just yesterday morning, when she woke to the aroma of the coffee he'd made and the breakfast he'd cooked, she just might have held all she'd ever wanted in the palm of her hand.

But she'd tossed it away.

Or had she?

She wouldn't blame J.R. if he never wanted to see her again. But she had to try to set things to right, even if it was just to share what was in her heart.

Determined to speak to him tonight, she started to

change out of her sweats, but thought better of it. What was she trying to prove with the stylish clothes, the bright colors, the pizzazz…?

She would go to him just as she was. Plain and vulnerable.

Honest.

But she'd better call a cab. No need taking any chances, even if she'd only had a single glass of wine.

While waiting for the driver to pick her up, she packed a few things in an overnight bag, just in case she decided to stay. Then she gathered the pet supplies she would need.

"Rusty?" she called to the kitten.

He poked his head around the doorjamb.

"Come on, little buddy. You're going, too."

She probably ought to worry about how Baron and Rusty would get along. But, in reality, it was only J.R.'s reaction that was on her mind.

J.R. and Toby had managed to jerry-rig that pump and get it going again until they could order a replacement.

He'd seen the old foreman at the Double Crown use the same trick, and it had worked like a charm back then.

It was nice being a part of the solution.

Still, now that he'd gotten home and was getting dinner ready for one instead of two, a cloud of disappointment settled over him. Not just because Isabella was supposedly busy, but because he figured she'd be using that excuse on him time and again.

He also realized that, as good as the sex had been, it apparently hadn't been enough. Isabella was looking for something J.R. couldn't provide.

He heard a vehicle pull into the driveway and wondered who it could be at this hour. Frank and Evie weren't due back for hours. And Toby had driven to San Antonio to meet Sarah's parents.

The doorbell sounded, and he placed the pan on the stove, then set the oven mitts on the counter.

When he answered, he damn near blinked to make sure he wasn't imagining things…

There stood Isabella, her hair a bit windblown, her purse and a canvas tote bag draped over her shoulder. She held a bag of supplies in one hand and the kitten in the other.

In the yard, a cab was backing up and turning around, leaving her on his doorstep, it seemed.

"I'm sure dinner is long over," she said, "but I really need to talk to you. And since I didn't want to ask the cab driver to wait, I was wondering if Rusty and I could spend the night."

"You certainly can if you'd like to." He stepped aside and let her in, yet he refrained from asking which bedroom she wanted to take. Something told him it wouldn't be his.

Dressed in those gray sweats, she looked ready for bed. Had she purposely chosen something that wouldn't arouse him? If so, that was too bad. It hadn't worked. Every cell in his body was buzzing just to have her within arms' length.

Hell, with the way he felt about her, he'd find her sexy dressed in a spacesuit.

"Is Baron around?" she asked. "I'm not sure how he's going to like having the kitten here again."

"He's napping by the fireplace in the great room. And as far as the cat goes, I'm sure there'll be a little hissing and barking, but they'll work it out, as they did when I first brought Rusty home."

At least, he hoped they would. It could end up being a long night. But then again, maybe the cat and dog would work things out before J.R. and Isabella would.

"Can I get you something to drink?" he asked. "A glass of wine maybe?"

"Actually, I'd rather have water. I had a glass of wine earlier, which is why I took a cab."

He didn't ask where she'd been or who she'd had the wine with. At this point, it wasn't his business, even if he'd like it to be.

"Why don't you set up a place for Rusty in the guest room?" he suggested. "We can separate him and Baron if we need to. Then I'll meet you in the courtyard."

"All right. I brought his litter pan and a few of his favorite toys."

As she followed his suggestion, he went to the courtyard, where the table was still set for two. He lit the candles, then turned the music on low. No need to waste the ambience he'd so carefully planned. Of course, depending on what she'd come to say, the ambience might fall flat anyway.

Next, he went into the kitchen, where he took the salad out of the fridge. He removed the plastic wrap and carried the bowl to the table. Then he dished up the hot meal.

Moments later, the table was ready.

"Ooh," she said from the alcove. "It's really beautiful. I hadn't imagined it with candles lit and the lanterns glowing."

She turned, scanning the courtyard, where the water trickled into the fountain.

"It has a completely different feel at night," he said, "doesn't it?"

"You're right. I'm so glad we started the renovations here."

So was he. And no matter what happened this evening, he was glad to finally be able to share the finished product with her.

He pulled out her chair, and she took a seat. Then he joined her.

She looked at her plate, noting the tamales and enchiladas. Then she scanned the courtyard and furrowed her brow. "Is that Tejana music?"

He nodded. "I thought you might like it. Do you want me to turn the sound up a little louder?"

"Yes, but not right now. I'd like to tell you something first."

"Shoot." He sat back in his chair and braced himself for the let's-be-friends talk. Or maybe the it's-not-you-it's-me speech.

"Earlier this year," she said, "I made a detailed list of all the things I wanted in a man. To be honest, when I first met you, I didn't think you fit too many of them."

He wasn't sure where she was going with this, nor whether he was up for hearing why. His ego, which had always been strong, had hit a low point today.

"Even after I got to know you," she said, "I downplayed some of your finer qualities, convincing myself that things wouldn't work out between us."

So far, she was right. Things didn't seem to be working out at all, but he bit his tongue and waited her out.

"I have a confession to make, J.R. You were right. The chemistry between us is magic. Making love with you was beyond my wildest dreams."

A smile tugged at his lips. As far as he was concerned, that said a hell of a lot. Any of the other things were negotiable.

"I might even love you," she added.

The heaviness that had been dogging him this evening began to lift. "So what's the problem?"

She sat back in her seat and crossed her arms. "I know that you're an orchestrator. You make things happen. You see what needs to be done, and poof. People do your bidding, and things happen your way."

He didn't see a problem with that. "I'm sorry, Isabella. From my point of view, that should be an asset, not a liability."

"I'm sure you do see it that way. But I don't want to be controlled. I want to call the shots sometimes. And I want to know that my hopes and dreams—past, present and future—will be respected."

He reached across the table and placed his hand on top of hers. "I would never purposely try to steamroll over you or your desires. If I ever get carried away, all you have to do is tell me to back off."

"And you'll promise to do that?"

He cocked his head slightly and slid her a crooked smile. "Back off? Well, I'm not sure. It would depend,

I guess. But I'll always respect your wishes, always temper my opinion based on your advice, your desires. And that *is* a promise."

She didn't respond right away, and he wondered if he'd somehow blown it already. But he wasn't going to let her have free rein and expect him to bow down to her every dictate. In a good relationship, a man and a woman learned to compromise. He'd seen the way it worked in his parents' marriage, and he suspected that was something she'd missed seeing while she was growing up.

"I want you to know that I appreciated the birthday celebration. And I like what you've done here tonight. It's special, and it really touches my heart. But…"

"But what?"

"My stepfather loved my mother, but he called all the shots. She loved him, so she agreed. But I'm not about to live like that, no matter how much I care for a man."

"I wouldn't respect you if you kowtowed to me on everything I said or wanted."

She picked up her glass and took a sip of water.

"For the record," he added, "I've been planning this dinner since the first time I stepped foot in this house. I wanted to see you here, wanted to share it with you."

"You've been planning this dinner that long?"

He nodded. "I think I fell in love with you the very first time we met, Isabella. At Fiesta, with your beautiful tapestries and your incredible eye for color and beauty."

She glanced down at her sweats, picking at the material in the oversize shirt. When she looked up, she smiled. "I used to be uncomfortable when I'd go places with my stepdad and his children because I felt as though I didn't fit in. So I began to counteract that awful feeling by dressing in a way that said, 'Look at me. I'm someone to be respected, to be noticed.'"

"You can rest assured that I'd notice you anywhere and wearing anything. I don't care if you're in a used gunny sack or the latest beaded gown—you're one in a million, Isabella."

She flushed at the pleasure of his compliment. "Thank you, J.R."

While he finished his salad, he realized that he had an admission to make. Because part of what she'd said had been true. He might have wanted to please her with the decorating job, the birthday party, even this dinner. But he'd had ulterior motives. Good ones, to be sure. Still, he'd tried to persuade her to do what he'd wanted her to.

"I have an apology to make," he finally admitted. "I thought that I could get you to see things my way. And I realize that I was wrong."

He glanced across the table, wondering if she would accept his apology.

"How were you wrong?" Isabella asked.

Was he realizing that he'd made a mistake by thinking he cared for her? Had her confession somehow diminished her in his sight?

"I love you, Isabella. And while I suspect that we're both strong-willed, I believe in compromise." He took the hand he'd been covering, turned it over and gave it a gentle squeeze. "More than anything, I'd like for the two of us to make a commitment tonight, but I understand if you're not ready. So I'll step back and let you take things at your own pace."

She'd made a list, but she'd used it to shield herself, to keep her from getting in too deep, from risking her heart. But the only way to freely love, was to open her heart and give love a chance. And that's just what she intended to do.

J.R., she realized, was the man she'd been looking for, the man she'd been hoping for. Her heart filled with so much joy that she thought it would spill over.

"I'd like to make that commitment now," she said.

"Nothing would make me happier."

J.R. stood, took her into his arms and kissed her. She kissed him right back, relishing the love that had been there all along.

When her legs were ready to buckle from his sweet assault of her mouth, he took her hand and led her to the master bedroom. "You wanted to start on the court-yard first, and you were right. It *is* the center of the house. But let's decorate this room next. I want it to reflect us both—our likes, our hopes, our dreams."

"There's nothing I'd like better."

They kissed again, and then he lifted her into his arms and placed her on the bed.

With the windows cracked open, and the background sounds of the ranch at rest, they made love—slowly at first, taking time to cherish the love they'd each declared for the other, the dreams that would take off tonight.

In the afterglow, as they lay wrapped in love, cele-brating the newness of their relationship, J.R. placed a lingering kiss on her brow. Then he slowly got out of bed and stood beside the nightstand.

She watched him open the top drawer, reach inside

and remove something small. When he returned to bed, he held a black, velvet-covered box that fit in his palm.

He handed it to her. "I have something for you."

"What's this?" she asked.

"Why don't you look and see?"

She opened it and saw a diamond ring. It wasn't especially large, but the stone sparkled as if it held all the magic in the world.

"It was my mother's," he said.

"It's beautiful."

"Before she died, she told me to look for my soul mate. She promised I'd find her. And I did. Marry me, Isabella. Be my wife, my best friend and my partner in life."

She didn't know what to say, but not from indecision. That was no longer her problem. Now her biggest struggle was in trying to wrap her heart around all the love flowing inside her.

"I love you, too, J.R. And I can't wait to marry you and start a family. I want a houseful of boys, just as your mother had. And I want them all to be like you."

A smile burst on his face, lighting up his eyes. "I'd like a couple of girls, too. Each one of them as pretty and as talented as their mama."

She withdrew the diamond that had once belonged to Molly Fortune.

"Let me," he said, as he took the ring from her and slipped it on the third finger of her left hand. "I love you, Isabella. And I promise to honor and protect you for the rest of my life. I can't wait to teach our children about their diverse heritage. And I can't wait to start a few new traditions of our own."

In her heart, she knew he would do whatever it took to keep that promise. And so would she. Their children would be unique individuals, yet part of a strong and rich heritage, a chain stretching back through generations.

Just as they sank back on the bed, ready to celebrate the love they'd just declared, the commitment they'd made, her cell phone rang.

She wanted to ignore the call and tell the world to go away, to leave them alone, but then she glanced at the display and recognized her father's number.

"I'd better get this," she said. "It's my dad."

"Uh-oh. Maybe I should have asked for your hand."

She smiled, then placed her index finger over her lips, shushing him. Her father didn't have to know that they'd had their honeymoon before J.R. had formally declared his intentions.

"Hi, Dad." She flashed a smile at J.R.

He made a little small talk at first, checking to see where she was. What she was doing. Then he went on to tell her why he'd called.

"I wanted to give you an update. I just heard through the grapevine that Roberto Mendoza received an urgent message from an anonymous caller, requesting a meeting with him at the Spring Fling and offering information he'd like to know."

Roberto was Isabella's cousin, the eldest son of José and Maria.

"*Mija*," her father added. "We don't know who's behind the threats that have been made or where they'll strike next. So please be careful."

Isabella looked at J.R., the man she loved. "I'm in good hands, Papa."

And she was.

Neither she nor J.R. knew what tomorrow might bring, but it really didn't matter. Together, they would face whatever the future might hold.

* * * * *

Look for the next installment of the new
Special Edition continuity
FORTUNES OF TEXAS: RETURN TO RED ROCK

Ross Fortune is bent on keeping his feelings to himself, even as he tries to clear his sister's name while caring for her teenage son. But when counselor Julie Osterman enters the picture, intent on helping Ross's nephew, the tough-as-nails private investigator falls for the beautiful woman. Has he finally found the one woman who can touch his heart?

Don't miss
FORTUNE'S WOMAN
by RaeAnne Thayne
On sale May 2009,
wherever Silhouette Books are sold.

Celebrate 60 years of pure reading pleasure
with Harlequin®!

Step back in time and enjoy a sneak preview of an
exciting anthology from Harlequin® Historical with
THE DIAMONDS OF WELBOURNE MANOR

This compelling anthology features three stories
about the outrageous Fitzmanning sisters. Meet
Annalise, who is never at a loss for words… But
that can change with an unexpected encounter in
the forest.

Available May 2009
from Harlequin® Historical.

"I'm the illegitimate daughter of notoriously scandalous parents, Mr. Milford. Candidates for my hand are unlikely to be lining up at the gates."

"Don't be so quick to discount your charms, my dear. Or the charm of your substantial dowry. Or even your brothers' influence. There are as many reasons to marry as there are marriages."

Annalise snorted. "Oh, yes. Perhaps I shall marry for dynastic reasons, or perhaps for property or influence. After all, a loveless, practical marriage worked out so well for my mother."

"Well, you've routed me on that one. I can think of no suitable rejoinder." Ned rose to his feet and extended his hand. "And since that is the case, let me be the first to wish you a long and happy spinster-hood."

Her mouth gaped open. And then she laughed.

And he froze.

This was the first time, Ned realized. The first time he'd seen her eyes light up and her mouth curl. The first time he'd witnessed her features melded together in glorious accord to produce exquisite beauty.

Unbelievable what a change came over her face. Unheard of what effect her throaty, rasping laughter had on his body. It pounded a beat upon his ear, quickly taken up by his pulse. It echoed through him, finally residing in his stirring nether regions.

So easily she did it, awakened these sensations within him—without any apparent effort at all. And she had called him potentially dangerous? Clearly the intelligent thing for him to do would be to steer clear, to leave her to the tender ministrations of Lord Peter Blackthorne.

"You were right." She smiled up at him as she took his hand and climbed to her feet. "I do feel better."

Ah, well. When had he ever chosen the intelligent path?

He did not relinquish her hand. He used it to pull her in, close enough that he could feel the warmth of her. "At the risk of repeating Lord Peter's mistake and anticipating too much—may I ask if you'll be my partner in battledore tomorrow?"

Her smiled dimmed. Her breath came a little faster. His own had gone shallow, as if he'd just run a race—and lost. He ran his gaze over the appealing lift of her brow and the curious angle of her chin. His index finger twitched.

"I should like that," she said.

His finger trembled again and he lifted it, traced the pink and tender shell of her ear, the unique sweep of her jaw. Her pulse leaped beneath her skin, triggering his own. Slowly he tilted her chin up, waiting for her to object, to step back, to slap his hand away.

She did none of those eminently sensible things. Which left him free to do the entirely impractical thing.

Baby soft, the skin of her lips. Her whole body trembled when he touched her there.

He leaned in. Her eyes closed, even as she stood straight against him, strung as tight as a bow. He pressed his mouth to hers. It was a soft kiss, sweet and chaste. And yet he was hot and hard and as ready as he'd ever been in his life.

She drew back a little. Sighed. Their breath mingled a moment before she slowly backed away.

"Oh," she breathed. Her dark eyes were full of wonder and something that looked like fear. He took a step toward her, but she only shook her head. His outstretched hand fell to his side as she turned to disappear into the wood. This was the first time, Ned realized. The first time, since he'd come to the house party at Welbourne Manor, that he'd seen her eyes light up.

* * * * *

*Follow Ned and Annalise's story in May 2009 in
THE DIAMONDS OF WELBOURNE MANOR
Available May 2009 from Harlequin® Historical*

We'll be spotlighting a different series
every month throughout 2009
to celebrate our 60th anniversary.

Look for Harlequin® Historical in May!

Celebrations begin with
a sumptuous Regency house party!

Join three scandalous sisters in

**THE DIAMONDS OF
WELBOURNE MANOR**

Glittering, scintillating, sensual fun
by Diane Gaston, Deb Marlowe
and Amanda McCabe.

60 years of Harlequin,
600 years of romance
in Harlequin Historical!

You're invited to join our Tell Harlequin Reader Panel!

By joining our new reader panel you will:

- Receive Harlequin® books—they are FREE and yours to keep with no obligation to purchase anything!
- Participate in fun online surveys
- Exchange opinions and ideas with women just like you
- Have a say in our new book ideas and help us publish the best in women's fiction

In addition, you will have a chance to win great prizes and receive special gifts! See Web site for details. Some conditions apply. Space is limited.

To join, visit us at
www.TellHarlequin.com.

REQUEST YOUR FREE BOOKS!

2 FREE NOVELS PLUS 2 FREE GIFTS!

SPECIAL EDITION®

Life, Love and Family!

YES! Please send me 2 FREE Silhouette Special Edition® novels and my 2 FREE gifts (gifts are worth about $10). After receiving them, if I don't wish to receive any more books, I can return the shipping statement marked "cancel." If I don't cancel, I will receive 6 brand-new novels every month and be billed just $4.24 per book in the U.S. or $4.99 per book in Canada. That's a savings of at least 15% off the cover price! It's quite a bargain! Shipping and handling is just 25¢ per book*. I understand that accepting the 2 free books and gifts places me under no obligation to buy anything. I can always return a shipment and cancel at any time. Even if I never buy another book from Silhouette, the two free books and gifts are mine to keep forever.

235 SDN EEYU   335 SDN EEY6

Name	(PLEASE PRINT)	
Address		Apt. #
City	State/Prov.	Zip/Postal Code

Signature (if under 18, a parent or guardian must sign)

Mail to the **Silhouette Reader Service:**
IN U.S.A.: P.O. Box 1867, Buffalo, NY 14240-1867
IN CANADA: P.O. Box 609, Fort Erie, Ontario L2A 5X3

Not valid to current subscribers of Silhouette Special Edition books.

Want to try two free books from another line?
Call 1-800-873-8635 or visit www.morefreebooks.com.

* Terms and prices subject to change without notice. Prices do not include applicable taxes. Sales tax applicable in N.Y. Canadian residents will be charged applicable provincial taxes and GST. Offer not valid in Quebec. This offer is limited to one order per household. All orders subject to approval. Credit or debit balances in a customer's account(s) may be offset by any other outstanding balance owed by or to the customer. Please allow 4 to 6 weeks for delivery. Offer available while quantities last.

Your Privacy: Silhouette is committed to protecting your privacy. Our Privacy Policy is available online at www.eHarlequin.com or upon request from the Reader Service. From time to time we make our lists of customers available to reputable third parties who may have a product or service of interest to you. If you would prefer we not share your name and address, please check here. ☐

SSE.

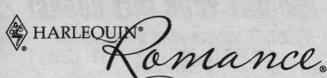

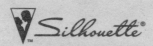

COMING NEXT MONTH

Available April 28, 2009